The
WILD
PATH

SARAH R. BAUGHMAN

Ⓛ Ⓑ
LITTLE, BROWN AND COMPANY
New York   Boston

Copyright © 2020 by Sarah R. Baughman
Excerpt from *The Light in the Lake* copyright © 2019 by Sarah R. Baughman

Cover art copyright © 2020 by David Dean. Cover design by Jenny Kimura. Cover copyright © 2020 by Hachette Book Group, Inc.

Little, Brown and Company
Hachette Book Group
1290 Avenue of the Americas, New York, NY 10104
Visit us at LBYR.com

Originally published in hardcover and ebook by Little, Brown and Company in September 2020
First Trade Paperback Edition: October 2021

Little, Brown and Company is a division of Hachette Book Group, Inc. The Little, Brown name and logo are trademarks of Hachette Book Group, Inc.

The publisher is not responsible for websites (or their content) that are not owned by the publisher.

The Library of Congress has cataloged the hardcover edition as follows:
Names: Baughman, Sarah R., author.
Title: The wild path / Sarah R. Baughman.
Description: First edition. | New York : Little, Brown and Company, 2020. | Audience: Ages 8–12. | Summary: Twelve-year-old Claire struggles to cope while her eighteen-year-old brother, Andy, is treated for drug addiction and her family prepares to sell her beloved horses, but finally accepts that change can be good.
Identifiers: LCCN 2019056786 | ISBN 9780316422475 (hardcover) | ISBN 9780316422444 (ebook) | ISBN 9780316422451 (ebook other)
Subjects: CYAC: Brothers and sisters—Fiction. | Horses—Fiction. | Drug addiction—Fiction. | Rehabilitation—Fiction. | Family life—New Hampshire—Fiction. | New Hampshire—Fiction.
Classification: LCC PZ7.1.B378 Wil 2020 | DDC [Fic]—dc23
LC record available at https://lccn.loc.gov/2019056786

ISBNs: 978-0-316-42243-7 (pbk.),
978-0-316-42244-4 (ebook)

Printed in the United States of America

CW

10 9 8 7 6 5 4 3 2 1

TO MATTHEW, MY PARTNER ON THE PATH

CHAPTER 1

Walking to our mailbox always feels longer than walking back. I take the same path both ways, past fields and fence line, but steps can't measure how fast I want to get there. It's the wanting, not the distance, that matters.

Everything around me is set to change. The maples covering the mountains started to pop, little bursts of red, yellow, and orange poking through green. I saw my breath this morning, a puff of smoke. The wind smells almost like snow.

And when I wrap my sweatshirt tight, the envelope pressed to my chest crinkles like dry leaves.

Dear Andy,
 Guess what?

That's how my letters always start. They're not like texts, where you get right to the point. There's more waiting. Not only in the time it takes to stretch whole sentences across a blank page, but in the trip that page takes from my desk to our mailbox and all the way to the Starshine Center in New Hampshire, where Andy can pick up a pen and write back.

I can't text him anyway, even though Mom and Dad got me a phone for my birthday this month, one of those simple ones with no apps at all, only their numbers and my best friend Maya Gonzalez's already programmed in. Andy doesn't have a number anymore. His cell phone's just one thing they took away, and they won't give it back until he's done with what they want him to do, until he figures out how to get better. "Getting better" is probably like walking to the mailbox—wanting to reach somewhere so bad but no matter how hard you try, you feel like you're wading through fallen leaves.

Still, I like Andy the way he is—how he wears his baseball cap crooked and sets up a tent in two minutes flat and pretends to steal my nose with his finger and thumb even though I'm twelve and he just turned eighteen. Will he still do those things once the Starshine Center has made him new?

Mom thinks Andy's homesick, even though he never says it. "He misses things we take for granted," she tells me, knotting her fingers together, her eyebrows pinching into that space above her nose that's always wrinkled now. "Tell him about those things." So I write: Sunny sneezed while I was brushing her face so now I have horse-hair AND snot all over my shirt.

I write what I know will make him smile. Because even though he wasn't doing much of it by the time he left, Andy loves smiling.

Proof: His letters back always start with a joke.

WHAT DO RACEHORSES EAT?

He hides the answer, written upside down at the end, to keep me reading. It's not like he has to—I already hold each of his words in my head as carefully as I hold Dad's homemade anise candies on my tongue, trying to make them last.

LOVE,
ANDY

P.S. Fast food!

It's bright today, and a little cold; stalks of corn shiver and shine like the sea. But the air feels good too, so I tip my head back and squint into the blue. I was born on a morning like this. That's how I got my name: Claire. In French, it means "bright and clear." "That's what you were from the beginning," my parents always say. "You still are."

They don't see how my insides flutter when I think about Andy, or school, or how to keep Sunny and Sam safe in our barn instead of sending them to a new one.

They don't see the birds in there.

Sparrows that soar over our barn can actually fly to the tops of clouds, then plunge back to earth. And that's exactly what my flutter feeling is like: It sweeps in from a place beyond me and gets under my skin, shaky as wings.

I don't know exactly where my sparrows go when they leave. But they visit more and more now that Andy's gone.

By the time I get to the mailbox, my hair's tangled under my chin. I brush it back, pull the metal door until it squeaks open, slip the letter in. Next comes my favorite part. It was Andy's favorite too. He was the one who explained we had to tip the red flag up with our fingers so that Mr. Meyer, who's been driving mail around our back roads since Mom was my age, knew he needed to stop and take what we'd left inside.

Dad says we used to fight over who got to put up the flag, but by the time my memory kicks in,

Andy was already letting me do it every time, lifting me at the waist so I could reach as high as I needed.

I raise myself a little on my toes now, even though I don't need to anymore, and push the flag up myself.

Dear Andy, I wrote this time.

Guess what? I miss you.

CHAPTER 2

"Back from the barn already?" Dad's frying eggs and potatoes at the stove. He doesn't need to turn around to know I'm on the front porch, stamping driveway dirt from my boots.

"Just mailed a letter. Came back for my hat." I grab it out of the basket by the door and tuck it over my ears.

In the living room, Mom pushes her chair back from the desk. She's spent a lot of time there lately, staring at the computer, looking for jobs. But now she bends her head around the doorway to the kitchen and wags her finger at me. "Told you it was cold."

I hold up my hands. "You might have been right. *This* time."

Mom laughs, then wraps her hands around the mug of coffee Dad offers. She sighs, and the wrinkles that scrunch up her forehead go soft and smooth. "Just what I needed," she says. Dad kisses her on the cheek.

"Ugh." I push the door halfway open. "See you guys later."

"We know not to wait." Dad stretches a set of metal tongs toward me, and I grab the strip of bacon hanging from them before heading back outside. Saturday breakfasts are always the best because Dad uses cooking as a way to procrastinate before settling into his living room chair with stacks of history essays to grade. He says food always turns out just the way he expects it to, unlike most other things in life.

Still, I'd rather keep my plate warm in the oven and take my time with morning chores. I can't ever squeeze enough minutes out of school days to groom Sunny and Sam with the currycomb plus both the hard and soft brushes, or to smear baby oil over the burrs tangled in their tails. But on weekends, time widens somehow.

Now I want to stretch it even further. Ever since Mom lost her accounting job when Kroller's Auto closed last spring, she and Dad have been worried. He teaches, and does tutoring in the summer, but it doesn't feel like enough. They both say it doesn't make much sense to keep horses anymore.

Dad says he's sorry. Mom says it will hurt her too. But they still hope to sell before winter comes, so they must not see how Sunny and Sam hold my skin and bones together, all in one piece. They don't see my heart quiet and calm when I'm braiding manes and picking hooves and squeezing my heels against soft flanks, pushing to go faster, cold wind in my hair.

There's always warmth in the barn. I slip into the hush of it and let my eyes adjust to the gray light of the big, airy entry that holds our hay wagon and tractor. From behind the latched door leading to the separate area we call the "horse stable," lined with stalls and a tack room, I hear Sunny and Sam shifting on their bedding, pushing wood shavings into piles with their big hooves.

When I walk past their stalls, they swing around to face me and hang their heads over the doors. I twist the strands of their chestnut forelocks in my hands and bring both my curved palms to their noses. Their whiskers tickle my skin.

Sam's a little bigger than Sunny, and a little sweeter too. When I move into his stall to get his feed bucket off its hook, he sways to the side, ears flopping, eyes half shut. Sunny has more opinions. She nods her big head up and down and noses my palm.

"Don't be rude," I say. I push my shoulder against hers until she scoots and I can pull her bucket out too.

The fact is, I love them both.

Today I'm riding Sam. A few days ago I worked Sunny on the lunge line, guiding her in circles, making her trot and canter. If I don't give her enough practice out of the saddle she gets prickly, shy. Holding a horse's attention while you're standing on the ground makes riding sessions work better.

But it's easy to get lazy and skip lunging Sam. No matter how many too-busy weekdays keep us away from our trails in the woods, Sam stays calm. If anything, he needs an extra nudge to get past a walk. When Maya comes to visit, she likes to ride him. She can't have a horse at her house in town, but she says being friends with me is close enough.

"Sam's more my style," she told me last time. "I bet he even likes to sleep in, just like I do." Then she leaned back, closed her eyes, and fumbled around for an imaginary snooze button. Maya always knows how to make me laugh.

I shake dust from a thick woven saddle pad, then bring out the saddle and bridle. Each piece has a name: horn, cantle, stirrup, cinch, headpiece, broadband, throatlatch, bit. Leather locks with metal and fits just right.

Sam follows me out of his stall, his nose at my elbow. Once I fasten cross-ties on either side of his halter I brush his thickening coat. I'm hurrying, filled with a tremor that's nothing like the sparrows. Instead of feeling like I'm going to break apart, I'm putting myself back together.

I work my fist between the saddle pad and the bony ridge of Sam's withers like Andy showed me, making a space where nothing pinches. Then I hook the right stirrup over the horn, swing the saddle up and set it gently down, pull the cinch swinging under Sam's belly, then tighten it. Next the bridle: bit slipping between teeth, reins gathered in my hands.

And then we're ready, gone, out into sunshine made more blinding by the barn's dimness. I blink slashes of light away and lead Sam down the path to our arena. It only has two walls front and back, with open-air sides, but the roof keeps too much rain and snow from getting in. We have a tiny circle I can ride in by myself well into the winter if I can't convince anyone else to trail ride, since I'm not allowed to do that alone. It's better than nothing. Every time I start moving Sam around the arena, I can see the hoofprints we left from last time leading the way.

"Ready, Sam?" I tighten the cinch one more time, then latch my left foot into the stirrup and swing my right over his back. Settle in. Here we go.

From the saddle, I see so much: the middles of

mountains, the mailbox a little speck in the dis- tance, its red flag the size of a pinprick. Every- thing on the ground looks smaller, matters less. My shoulders roll back, my muscles shift. Inside, I'm warm and strong.

Heels down, reins clutched in my gloves, eyes pointed straight ahead to where I'm going, I can do anything.

When I lead Sam back into the barn, I see Mom there, brushing Sunny. She's been coming to the barn during my chore time more often lately.

"Hey, you," she says. "Thought we could exer- cise both horses together, head out into the woods a bit. That way you can eat breakfast sooner."

Mom knows I can wait for breakfast. She's here for the same reason I am: because the barn's dark enough to make dirt look pretty, quiet enough for a crowded brain to think, softer to look at than a glowing screen. Because problems sink through the grooves in these wood-plank walls and get swallowed whole.

My heart swells a little. Maybe riding Sunny and Sam will remind Mom that they need to stay here.

Mom must see the hope rise into my cheeks, all rosy and warm, because she's gentle when she says, "We talked about this, Claire. We need to take care of Sunny and Sam as long as we still have them, and that includes exercise."

I feel the sparrows race in then, pecking my swelled-up heart. They tickle my throat, making it hard to talk. *I'm losing everything that matters*, a voice inside me whispers. *And I'll never get it back*.

Sunny and Sam aren't supposed to belong to anyone else. They're ours. And I don't care if Mom says I can still ride her friend Marcy's horse anytime. It's not the same.

"I already rode Sam," I mumble. "In the arena."

"It can't have been for very long, though," Mom says. "A little more won't hurt. And Dad's got so much grading to do. I'll never be able to drag him out here. You'll come, right?"

I always want to go into the woods. This is the best time of the year for it, the bugs finally gone and the damp smell of fresh leaves turning all around, mixing with the spice of cedar and pine.

When crisp air fills my lungs, it stills the sparrows too. I smile just thinking about it, and Mom sees.

"I'll take that as a yes." She rubs Sunny's neck and unclips the cross-ties. "This girl's all set. Ready to go?"

Mom leads Sunny toward the door, and I turn Sam around to follow.

"When do you think Andy will be home?" I whisper against his neck. "Not too long, huh?"

It seems like he's been gone forever, but Mom marks the days with Xs on the feed-company calendar she tacked on the barn wall, so I know it's really only been a month. August 27. That day, I followed Andy out of the car and up the steps of the Starshine Center, my tongue a block of ice refusing to melt in all that summer heat, keeping words too far down to speak while everything inside—my throat and ribs and flip-flopping stomach—screamed at him not to go. I knew why he was there. We had already sat down as a family the week before and I'd listened to Mom and Dad explain. Andy's voice cracked as he told me himself that there was such a thing as too much medicine, that he needed help to stop taking the pain pills a doctor had prescribed after he hurt his back snowmobiling. He'd taken too many, for too long. I understood what the therapists told us, that Andy has a problem he'll need to work on, that it's called *addiction*. I remembered how empty Andy's eyes had started to look, how he'd been staying out later and later at night and sometimes didn't come home at all. But I also knew that wasn't the real Andy. It couldn't be. When we camped on Pebble Mountain, he brought graham crackers and marshmallows and bars of chocolate. He lit fires without matches and whittled sticks to sharp points. He didn't need pills.

Sam looks at me from sleepy eyes, his ears flopping every which way. He's relaxed. I cup my hands under his nose, and he breathes into them, his whiskers tickling my palms.

He doesn't have any answers for me.

But with horses, and questions, you have to be patient.

CHAPTER 3

As I'm leading Sam toward the arena, my phone buzzes with a text. I stop, squint at the screen.

Whatcha up to?

It's Maya. When I'm talking to her, or even just listening, the same peaceful feeling I get in the barn works its way in and holds on. I slow down. The sparrows flit away. Now my breath fogs the tiny screen as I type back.

Trail ride w/ mom.

It won't be what Maya wants to hear. On weekends when she and I can get someone to drive us over to the other's house, we hang out. Not today, though. Dad won't want to leave his "grading chair" until every last essay's marked, which won't happen until dinner's gone cold, and Mom already said she needed to ramp up her job search over the weekend.

You didn't invite me?! 😠

Sorry! We only have 2 horses lol

Maya and I have known each other for a long time. Our moms are friends, and when we were little they used to let us both sit on Sam while they led us around the ring, over and over again.

Even back then, we were already pretty different. Not in the deep-down ways that actually make friendships stick. It's just that Maya used to toddle up to any kid on the playground and start babbling while I hung back, digging into the sand under the slide and narrowing my eyes at anyone who came close.

I'm glad we're not the same. It's kind of like Mom says: We complement each other. "You remind me of companion plants in a garden," she explained once. "Lettuce and tomatoes. Radishes and carrots. Different enough that when you're close together, you help each other out. Give each other space to grow."

Now, from the edge of the arena, Sam and I watch Mom work on the lunge line with Sunny, stepping in toward her flank and spinning the rope to make her change directions. Mom's been working with horses since she was my age, and she started teaching Andy about them as soon as he could walk. As he got older and Mom got busier with work, Andy started teaching me. But even though I've had a lot of practice, I can always learn something from watching Mom. Today it's how quickly she lets the rope slide through her hands to make Sunny turn. Her brain's always running a few steps ahead of Sunny's hooves.

Mom begins shortening the rope, letting Sunny slow and stop, then spin to face her.

"She looks tired," I say.

Mom laughs. "That was barely anything." She rubs Sunny's nose and leads her out of the arena, toward me and Sam. "It's just her mind working. That pretty much tires anyone out."

I settle into the saddle while Mom unclips the lunge line.

"So you sent another letter to your brother this morning?" Mom's looking very carefully at Sunny's bridle instead of at me now, pretending to adjust the straps even though Sunny's the only one who ever wears it.

"Yeah." She knows I went out to the mailbox already, and what else would I have been doing? What she *really* wants to know is what I wrote in the letter. Or what I think he'll write back. But I don't want to tell her—the letters are only for Andy and me.

Mom really loves the Starshine Center. The whole drive back from dropping Andy off, she kept saying, "Didn't that place have such a nice *feel*?" and "I know it'll be great for him." I pressed my forehead against the window and closed my eyes to erase the sounds. Dad just nodded, his fingers tight on the steering wheel. It started raining as we drove and he had to turn the windshield wipers on high to scatter fat drops like tears. Once I heard him say, "It's a shot, anyway. Let's hope he takes it," but that was all.

"I'm sure he loves getting your letters." Mom takes Sunny's reins in her palms and turns to face me. She wants me to keep writing, to help Andy "get better." But I think what he needs most is to come home.

All the hope in Mom's voice brings the sparrows sweeping down, their wings rustling over my ribs. I turn Sam toward the woods, let the sun blind me again.

We're lucky to live right past Pebble Mountain, with paths cutting straight through eighty acres of mixed forest. Mom likes to remind me that these trees have been stretching up to the sky since before her mom was my age. She says trees show people how long it takes a thing to grow, and how long it can last. She doesn't talk as much about how quickly it can get taken away.

"Perfect weather," Mom says, changing the

subject as she swings onto Sunny's back. "Cold, but not too cold. Sun's shining. Couldn't ask for a better day to get out there, right?"

Mom goes in front even though Sunny has her ears pricked forward so far I can see the veins in them popping out. She's not like Sam, who couldn't care less where he goes or who he's with. Sunny doesn't want to be alone, and even when she's with another horse, she has a hard time leading. Some horses are just like that: nervous about being in charge. It's hard to cure them of it. The idea, though, is to keep practicing so Sunny gets a little more independent on the trail.

Beyond the pasture, we turn toward the stand of pines that brings us into the woods. Green rises all around, mixed with the turning maples, and I take deep breaths of sweet air. Sam moves slowly, each step calm and measured. In the spaces between trees, I see indentations in the dirt: hollows that look a lot like hoofprints. I lean a little closer, then shake my head. It can't be what it looks like. These woods belong to us—the closest neighbors with animals live miles away. And when we ride here, we don't weave around the trees. Deer must have come through—big ones, with tracks that widened over time.

"Sunny's doing good," Mom says over her shoulder. And I can see that even though Sunny's ears are still pricked forward, her head's down just a bit; she's not looking frantically around for something to run away from.

"Sam's trying to keep up," I call. That makes Mom laugh.

We don't talk about how Andy isn't here. How if he had been, he would have been riding Sunny instead. He'd have strapped a small thermos to the saddle horn so he could let me sneak tastes of his "mountain coffee" blazing hot and sweet with cream and extra maple syrup. I can almost hear Andy laughing at one of his own corny jokes, the sound bouncing off tree bark. *Why did the pine tree get in trouble? Because it was being knotty!*

Andy's laughter always sounded extra-loud because of how much quieter the woods get in fall. Sometimes a branch cracks. Other times a wood thrush calls. If you're walking, you can hear your boots rustle in dry leaves or squish in mud. When snow finally comes, always by the beginning of November but usually earlier, it has a swelling silence that goes over everything.

The trail starts to widen, and Mom motions me up next to her. I have to squeeze with my legs and dig my heels a little bit into Sam's side to convince him that matching Sunny's pace is a good idea. But Sam always listens, even when he doesn't want to.

"Listen, Claire," Mom says quietly, looking down at her reins. "I know this isn't an easy subject, but...I think we need to discuss it again. I can tell you've been having a hard time accepting what needs to happen."

She doesn't have to actually say the words about selling Sunny and Sam for me to know what she means.

"I still don't get it." I shake my head. "How hard is it to keep them?"

"Honey," Mom says. "I know I've already explained the costs involved in owning horses. Not just the food and tack and supplies, but vet and farrier bills too."

When there's no right thing to say, sometimes it's better to stay quiet, and I do.

Mom keeps going. "Plus, the barn needs repairs. Pretty big ones. And horses don't make money; they take it. Especially with Andy at Starshine—"

She stops then, but my mind fills in the rest. I know the Starshine Center isn't cheap. I've listened to Mom and Dad talk in low voices about loans and interest and bills. But if Andy comes home soon, like I know he will, it won't be an issue anymore.

"You're always telling me that nothing's permanent," I say, thinking of the calendar tacked on the barn wall. "So neither is Starshine. Andy won't be there forever."

"But losing my job is the other big piece of this," Mom says. "Andy can't fix that. We'll be paying for Starshine even after he comes home, and we can't guarantee when he'll leave either."

"You said before the snow comes." I can feel my voice growing wild, spinning away at a canter.

"Hopefully." Mom's voice wavers a little. "But I shouldn't have promised. It's hard to say for sure. It depends on...many factors."

I push her uncertainty away. "Well, when he does come home, things should be just like he remembers them," I say. "That way, he can go back to normal."

Mom sighs and pulls Sunny to a stop. "This is one change he'll just have to manage."

At Starshine, they say consistency is everything. When we first brought Andy there, one of the therapists explained that when people are working to overcome addiction, regular routines are important. She talked about how Andy would need to develop "coping strategies" he could use when he got back home, like managing stress and avoiding risky situations. But how will Andy cope with anything if Sunny and Sam aren't here?

"This isn't easy for me either, Claire," Mom continues. Her voice sounds like it's slipped underwater. "You know I grew up with horses. I wouldn't do this if I—" She shakes her head then and sets Sunny back in motion. I follow.

That's why you should understand, I think. *And why you shouldn't make all these changes that are too big and strange.*

But the words stick in my throat, making the

sparrows flock and flutter. I close my eyes quickly, then look past Mom, into the trees.

That's when I spot it.

Just a wisp at first. The curl of a black tail, vanishing in clustered leaves as soon as my eyes grab on to what they're seeing. Then a hoof, pawing the ground. But when I look up to find the rest of the leg, and the body, it's gone, the impression it left already filling back in.

Sam's ears are pricked so far forward I can see the veins crisscrossing up from base to pointed tip. Ahead of me, Sunny's nodding her head up and down, twisting her reins and sidestepping.

A sheaf of mane, rippling like a wave.

A dappled gray back, running straight across, then rounding and curving down.

It doesn't make sense. My mind can't trust my eyes. Still, I know there's something moving between the trees.

A horse.

It can't be a horse. The only horses in these woods are Sunny and Sam, and that's only when we're guiding them through.

Mom's looking down at Sunny's withers instead of into the space between the trees where the tail and hoof slipped through.

"Hey," she says, glancing quickly at me. "What's gotten into these two? Even Sam looks nervous." She shakes her head, turning Sunny in a small tight circle, hushing her. "Guess I let her get too comfortable. Let's trot a little, then head back."

As Mom nudges Sunny forward I turn my head to the left, right, looking for something. For any sign that what I saw was real.

Now we're moving faster down the trail, too fast to stop for dappled backs and hints of hooves. Still, every part of my body feels rock-heavy, like it wants to dig in, go back to where we came from and keep looking for what I know I saw.

CHAPTER 4

In school on Monday I stare at a crack in the table I share with Maya, trying to figure out how to slip her a note about the strange horse in the woods. At the front of the room, Ms. Larkin reminds us about the History Fair next month, her hands gesturing every which way as she tries to get us to feel as thrilled about it as she does.

The History Fair happens every year. We have to do research—the specific topic changes every year—and give a presentation in front of an audience of community members. Adults. Just thinking about that draws the sparrows from their hiding places, and I feel my heart thump against their shaking wings.

"This year we're doing things a little differently," Ms. Larkin says.

That doesn't sound good. I like Ms. Larkin, but she looks dangerously excited right now. She clicks the projector on, and a meme flashes onto the whiteboard—an actor who looks sort of familiar, hunched into a weird-looking car. **Back 2 What?** it says in thick white type.

The meme is typical. Ms. Larkin starts pretty much every class with one that relates, even just a little, to whatever we're doing. She insists that they're a "fascinating form of evolving digital literacy," whatever that means. Leave it to Ms. Larkin to make something cool sound dorky, but she does have pretty decent taste in memes. She's made a few of them herself, and they're actually funny.

"I realize I'm old," Ms. Larkin says, clutching her head like she's in pain and squashing her hair. "But please, someone, tell me you've heard of this movie."

Maya and I look at each other, shrug. Nobody says anything. There are fifteen of us in class, and most of us started kindergarten together here at Pebble Village School. A few have come and gone, but for the most part, we've been stuck together for a while. The way I see it, that ends up being both good and bad. Good because of Maya, who sits with me at lunch and whispers secrets without needing me to talk. Bad because everyone else thinks I'm shy and that's it. In two years, we'll all get on a bus and go to the regional high school where Dad teaches, with kids from five other towns, and even though Mom tells me it will be good to "expand my horizons," I haven't been ready to think about it yet.

Cory, two tables away, shoots his hand in the air. "Got it!"

Ms. Larkin smiles. "Okay, let's see how well-versed you are in eighties films," she says. She looks around the room and wags a finger in the air. "The rest of you, pay close attention. Tonight, look this up on Netflix. Required viewing."

Maya rolls her eyes, but she's looking back and forth between the screen and Cory, waiting. "Wait, did she just tell us to watch Netflix for homework?" she whispers.

Cory slams his hand down on the table. *"Back to the Future,"* he says.

"Thank you!" Ms. Larkin reaches her arms out wide and strikes the air like she won something. "A cinematographic masterpiece. Cory, can you explain the premise of the movie?"

Cory runs his hand through his curly hair. "So there's this scientist, right? He figures out how to travel back in time. And this kid Marty goes back in time with him, but things get all messed up and then he has to go *back* to the future to fix them. Get it?"

"Perfect." Ms. Larkin clicks to the next slide. The meme's gone, replaced by a bulleted list under the title **Back, Then to the Future**.

"We think of history as being over and done with," Ms. Larkin says. "But *I—*" She raises an index finger, her eyes wide. "I am here to tell you it's definitely not. Cory: In the movie, how does history affect what happens in the present?"

"So, it's superweird," Cory says, turning in his

seat to face all of us. "When Marty goes into the past, he saves his dad from getting hit by a truck. Sounds like a good thing, right? But he actually shouldn't have, because it turns out getting hit was how his dad met his mom. So if Marty changes that one little thing, he won't even exist later!"

"Exactly. This movie suggests that even the smallest change in history can alter the present, which at the time the history was happening was also the future," Ms. Larkin says, tapping the bulleted list. "So in your projects for this year's fair, we'll focus on how a person, issue, or event from the past affects how we experience life today."

Jamila shifts in her seat. "Wait, how do we figure that out?"

"Good question," Ms. Larkin says. "Any historical topic can be relevant, if we look at it the right way. For example, think about women getting the right to vote. Instead of only presenting about when that happened and what they did, you can also show how women's issues inform current politics, or how the methods used during the suffrage movement have evolved to promote social justice."

Sometimes Ms. Larkin gets kind of carried away, but I think I understand what she means: look at history and show why it still matters.

It makes me think about Andy, and how much his past should matter. Isn't the Starshine Center trying to help people move beyond their pasts?

"Now, I've saved the best part for last: It's pretty exciting." Ms. Larkin clicks over to another meme: This one's a picture of a very large cat sitting on a pile of dollar bills. Giggles and groans erupt. "This year our local Rotary Club is offering a special prize to the student with the best speech."

"Actual money?" Cory leans forward, his eyes wide.

"Local judges from the community will vote on the presentations," Ms. Larkin says. "They're working with our rubric and looking for students who are both passionate and well-informed. It's not small change either: They're offering a five-hundred-dollar prize to the winner."

My heart pounds, a steady drum; I feel shaky, hollow. Five hundred dollars isn't enough to keep Sunny and Sam forever. But it could at least buy some hay to help get through the winter, which would give me more time to change Mom's and Dad's minds.

Outside the classroom windows, trees rustle in the wind. The colors get brighter every day, leaves weaving patchwork quilts. I think about the wisp of tail in the trees. The dappled gray back, almost blending in with rough bark and mottled branches, but not quite.

"Helloooo," Maya says. "Earth to Claire."

I look up. Ms. Larkin's clicked off the projector, and kids are pulling papers out of their notebooks.

"We're supposed to be brainstorming," Maya says. "Topics we're interested in. Historical connections and stuff."

"Do you know what you're doing?" I ask.

Maya always knows what she's doing. "Edna Beard. No question. First female Vermont legislator, and she totally kicked butt."

That doesn't surprise me. Maya's dad, Mr. Gonzalez, is a judge, and she always says she wants to work with the law somehow when she grows up.

"I totally want that prize," Maya says. "There's

this summer camp in Washington, DC, for girls who are interested in legal stuff and politics. But there's no way my parents would pay for all of it. This would help a lot."

The drumbeat in my chest gets louder. Maya *could* really use that prize money. But so could I.

Ms. Larkin clears her throat. "Remember, folks, if you're not sure where to start, try to work backward—think about what interests you have now. From there, I can help you look for historical connections."

Maya pushes a blank piece of paper my way. Interests we have now...for me, there's only one. And it doesn't have to do with history.

"You stuck?" Maya asks.

"Kind of." I pick up a pencil, doodle loops and squiggles on my paper.

Maya sighs. "It doesn't have to be perfect. You just need one idea."

She's trying to help me get started, but my eyes burn. "It's hard thinking about school when all that really matters to me is whether or not I can figure out a way to keep the horses."

Maya's lips twist in a frown. "Your parents are still talking about selling?"

I nod, tears blurring my eyes. "It's a sure thing now. By the time Andy gets home, Sunny and Sam might already be gone. It'll be so weird for him."

Maya looks down at her paper. "That stinks, Claire."

I shake my head. I want to tell her she doesn't need to be sorry, it's not her fault, but my throat feels thick and strange.

"How's it going over here, ladies?" Ms. Larkin kneels at our table. Not the greatest timing. She twirls a pencil in her hand.

Maya clears her throat. She can always tell when I don't want to have to keep talking. "So, I'm researching Edna Beard," she says, and starts telling Ms. Larkin all about what she already knows (which is a lot), and what she wants to learn (also, interestingly, a lot). That gives me time to think, though the only thoughts I have are images of the barn, of trees, of Sunny and Sam.

Part of the problem is that all we do with Sunny and Sam is ride. I know when Mom was younger, her dad kept horses who helped him log the forest, hauling wood that kept his house warm all winter. According to Mom, when she first got Sunny and Sam, Grandpa joked about making them useful somehow. "Put those horses to work!" he'd say. "I bet they're good for more than just trail riding."

"What's better than trail riding?" Mom had shot back. "Besides, Dad, most people don't use horses for logging. You were one of the last, back when I was growing up. And I was so little I don't even remember it."

"But those old ways might come back," Grandpa had said. After he died last winter, Mom's eyes looked sunset red and raw for months.

I wonder: If Mom and Dad started using Sunny and Sam in a practical way, like people used to, would we still need to sell them? Maybe *that's* how history could affect the present.

"And how about you, Claire?" Ms. Larkin asks.

Sparrows stir, and heat from their tiny wakening bodies rushes into my cheeks. I start to swallow but my tongue lodges against my teeth and I cough instead.

Maya slowly pushes her water bottle across the desk, her eyes never leaving my face. "She's been thinking about maybe researching how...," she says slowly, her voice turning up a little at the end, giving me time.

I tip the bottle back and let water run down my throat. The sparrows shake droplets off their heads, yet remain. Nobody else can sense them anyway, except Maya. And she always swoops in at exactly the right time.

"How people used to use horses," I blurt out. "A long time ago." I'm surprised by the sound of my voice, the loudness of it. And by the idea. But Maya's words helped me find mine, and this is a topic I could definitely get excited about.

Ms. Larkin nods and her eyebrows crinkle together. I can tell she's interested. "Isn't that something your family does? I remember you telling us that your grandfather used horses to harvest wood."

"Yeah, but he stopped a long time ago," I say. "I think it would be cool to learn about a time when everybody needed horses. Not just for logging, but for everything."

"I see potential there," Ms. Larkin says. "Remember the importance of looking into the future too. You could compare and contrast traditional farming methods that relied on horses with more modern approaches."

"You mean like machines," I say. Because that's exactly it. People don't need horses in the same way anymore. Everything's changed.

Maybe I can find a way for our family to change too, so we can keep Sunny and Sam. That way, once Andy's done at the Starshine Center, everything will be the way it's supposed to be.

"Nailed it," Maya whispers as Ms. Larkin moves to the next table. "Where'd that come from?"

But I can't explain it. The idea appeared suddenly, a horse moving quick and quiet through trees.

CHAPTER 5

When the school bus drops me off, I check the mailbox even though I know it's too early for Andy to have written. It took us a few tries, but we figured out that letters need exactly two days to go each way. Since I mailed mine on Saturday, and Sunday doesn't count because it's Mr. Meyer's day off from driving the mail truck, Andy probably won't even read what I wrote until tomorrow, let alone have time to write back.

But stuck in the middle of a rubber-banded stack of bills, coupons, and catalogs is a regular envelope with handwriting in the corner and a return address I know by now:

A. B.

STARSHINE CENTER

802 WHEELER ROAD

DOWNING, NH 05497

My breath catches. Andy wrote me just because he wanted to.

I open the envelope with shaking fingers.

WHAT DID ONE WALL SAY TO THE OTHER WALL?

I shake my head and smile, forcing myself not to look down at the answer.

YOU'RE PROBABLY WONDERING WHY YOU'RE GETTING AN EXTRA LETTER. WELL, WHAT CAN I SAY, LITTLE C.? SOMETIMES A BROTHER'S JUST GOTTA WRITE HIS SISTER.

I WAS THINKING ABOUT YOU ANYWAY, BECAUSE WE HAD OATMEAL WITH BROWN SUGAR AT BREAKFAST.

REMEMBER HOW MOM ONLY EVER LET US TAKE ONE
SPOONFUL OF SUGAR BUT I HID THE CONTAINER UNDER
THE TABLE AND DUMPED EXTRA ON WHEN SHE WASN'T
LOOKING?

I laugh. Andy and I pinkie-swore never to tell Mom about that. But he was the one with the guts to snatch the brown sugar in the first place. I've been eating single-scoop-of-sugar oatmeal ever since he left, and I don't even like it.

I'M GLAD THE COFFEE'S GOOD HERE. I HAVE TO
GET UP SO EARLY.

I used to be the one shaking him awake before school. "It's still dark!" he'd mutter when morning light started fading in fall and winter finally snuffed it out. "Who gets up in the dark? I'm telling you, it's unnatural."

I can picture the outline of Andy's days now like the frame of a house or bones under skin: just a structure, the rest empty. I know he has individual therapy in the morning and group therapy in the afternoon, some chores in between on the farm Starshine Center runs. Letters fill in the gaps.

> BUT NOW I HAVE AN HOUR BEFORE GROUP, AND IT'S
> BASICALLY SPACE-OUT TIME.

Space-out time for Andy means thinking time, when he gets the silence that makes his brain move and spin.

> REMEMBER WHEN WE USED TO DO SPACE-OUT TIME
> UP AT PEBBLE MOUNTAIN? I WAS TELLING MY FRIENDS
> MARIE AND DAMIAN ABOUT THAT. THIS IS JUST ABOUT
> THE RIGHT TIME OF YEAR TO HAUL SLEEPING BAGS UP
> FOR A LAST CHANCE TO WATCH STARS BEFORE THE
> SNOW COMES.

Of course I remember. We'd lie on cold ground and in all that quiet with nothing to do, nowhere else we had to be, Andy would stare, his eyes wide open, reflecting the light from the sky. But who are Marie and Damian?

You can still find your constellations, right? Great Bear, Little Bear, Orion's Belt—you'd better not forget those while I'm gone.

Andy used to tell stories too, like about Aquila, the eagle who carried Zeus's messages to humans far below the stars. "You know what, Little C.?" he told me once. "Sometimes I think Aquila might still be up there. I keep thinking if I look close enough I'll find her."

We'd stay awake so long up there, our eyes crawling over the dark night sky. I remember how it felt to slip onto the edge of sleep and find that same peace I got in the barn, the simple wholeness that told me everything was okay.

We haven't gone to Pebble Mountain for a long time.

I want Andy to write, *Wish I could be there right now!* But he doesn't.

I fold the letter back up without finishing. If I keep reading, it will be over too soon. This way I can save it for as long as I want. I'll wait until after my support group meeting.

On Monday afternoons, Dad always drives me to the community center over on Lincoln Street in Belding, which is more like a city than where we live, but still pretty small. It has a few stores and a bank, and Cedar Lake, but not much else. And that's okay with me. I don't need a lot of people around, wanting to ask questions about Andy. It's hard enough having to sit on folding chairs set up in a circle, listening to kids I don't know very well talking about their relatives as though their stories have anything to do with our family's.

But Mom and Dad say going to the support group is a good idea for now. "Just until Andy gets home," Mom said.

"Or maybe longer than that," Dad said. "You and the other kids have something in common, hon."

Why would Dad think I needed to keep going? The people kids talk about at those meetings—moms, dads, cousins, brothers, and sisters—they're not like Andy. They can't be.

Andy taught me how to build fires in the snow so we didn't have to wait until summer for s'mores.

Andy welded sheets of metal into a rack for storing firewood and gave it to Mom for her birthday last year. Andy ended up at Starshine Center because he got in a bad snowmobile accident and hurt his back and pills kept the pain away for so long that eventually he didn't know how to *not* take them. The problem was, when he kept taking pills, they started causing pain instead of relieving it. And they tricked him too, made him think he needed them more and more even though he had already stopped feeling better, even though we all could tell he felt worse—more sad, more tired, more hurt.

He has to stop taking them now. I know he will.

"These meetings don't really help," I tell Dad. I look out the window instead of at him. The mountains seem like they're on fire, warm colors all mashed together in the trees.

Dad sighs. "We've talked about this, Claire. It's important to share your feelings and your experience with other people."

I shake my head. "Nobody makes us talk if we don't want to."

Dad lets the steering wheel slide through his fingers and presses his lips together. "Give it time. It's only been a month."

He pulls up next to the front entrance and puts the truck in park. Silence fills the space between us, but it's not the comfortable space-out kind. It feels breakable and sharp, like glass. At least Dad's eyes don't have those little spears of hope Mom's do, like me walking into that community center will bring Andy back any faster. It won't. Which is why it's so confusing that he brings me in the first place.

"It's not like you and Mom go to any meetings for grown-ups," I say. "I don't know why I should have to go to these."

Dad shifts his eyes away from me, back to the steering wheel. He knows I'm right about that. He and Mom said they'd try, back when Andy first went to the Starshine Center and the staff member who showed us around stuffed pamphlets into their hands and told them the groups would be helpful, but they haven't yet.

I close the door a little harder than I need to,

and Dad rolls the passenger window down. "Pick you up in an hour?" he asks, leaning across the seat to be sure I'll hear.

I can't bring myself to just walk away, so I nod, but I'm not going to pretend like this is a good idea.

As soon as I'm inside, our group facilitator, Sharon, walks over. "It's good to see you again, Claire."

I let her shake my hand. "You too." Sharon's nice, but I can already feel sparrows hovering at my shoulder, wanting in.

The meeting room's pretty full, so I'll have to sit next to someone this time. Even though I saw a kid from my school attend once, I don't know most of the others. We'll end up at the same high school— some of the older kids are already there—but I'll keep my distance as long as I can. I don't want to be so close I could accidentally brush another person's elbow or see what color earrings they're wearing or hear them sniffle when they get sad.

I slip into the seat next to Nari, who's pretty quiet too. She smiles, and I manage to smile back, because it's more comfortable being around someone who doesn't make me feel like I need to talk. Not like Caleb and Anna, who share during every meeting. As soon as I hear their voices, my own seems even harder to find. They've been coming for a while, though, longer than I'll need to.

"Hi, everyone," Sharon says. "Welcome back. Let's get started."

At the beginning, we're all supposed to close our eyes and breathe for a moment. Sharon says it will help "center our thoughts," but mostly it makes me want to run away.

I peek my eyes open just long enough to glance at Nari. She looks so much more peaceful than I feel.

"Who would like to share?" Sharon has beautiful brown eyes, cedar-bark skin, and black hair clustered in waterfalls of curls. Even though I don't like talking at meetings, I like listening to her voice. It calms me, like the sound of tiny Pine Lake waves touching sand on a mostly still day.

The air hums, like it can hear all the words gathering.

Anna starts. "Mom hasn't drank yet. It's been—"

She looks up at the ceiling and taps her fingers. "Forty-two days. I'm proud of her. I mean, obviously. But also…" She pauses then, gathers strings of sandy hair in her snow-pale hands, brings it around her shoulder and tugs.

Nobody says anything. We're not really supposed to.

Anna looks down at her shoes, letting her hair fall around her face, and her cheeks puff out like she's not sure she wants to keep talking. In a way, it feels like I should cross the room, go up to her, and tell her something, anything to make her feel better, but Sharon says it's really important that we give each other time instead. Outside the community center, people don't always have the chance to say everything they want to say. "In here," Sharon told us, "we get all the time we need."

When Anna takes a deep breath, I can see how maybe even trying to comfort her might not really have worked. She *does* have more to share; she just needed time to get the words in order. I know how that goes.

"But I'm also scared. When I go to visit at her

apartment, I look in the cabinet where I know she kept those bottles, to make sure there aren't any left." Anna rubs her forehead. "I know I shouldn't do that, though. It's not like I can stop her, right? What am I going to do if I find something? Pour it out?" She pauses, shakes her head. "She'll just get more. I mean, if she wants to."

My throat catches. I remember Andy's pills. Part of me thought if I'd found them early enough, if I'd hidden them deep in the barn, he wouldn't have ended up at Starshine Center. But could I have really stopped him from doing what he wanted to do?

Then Anna looks back up at us. "I don't mean she *really* wants to," she says quietly. "She doesn't actually *want* to drink. It's just..." Her voice trails off.

Sharon nods gently. Silence grows.

"Addiction makes her do things she might not really want to do. I...wish it didn't." Anna takes a deep breath. "That's all for now."

"Thanks, Anna," we all say.

That part's important too. We listen, and then we thank whoever shared. Because it takes courage to share.

But Sharon always reminds us it takes courage just to be, too. She says even if all we do is come and sit, we're doing enough because we're doing what we can do.

I'm not sure I believe that. It seems like there's a lot more I could be doing, especially to make sure Andy goes back to being his regular self when he gets home.

Still, something Anna said about her mom tumbles in my mind: *Addiction makes her do things she might not really want to do.*

What does Andy want to do?

Five minutes before the meeting ends, Sharon looks up at the clock. "Thanks, all of you," she says. "Those who shared, and those who listened. I'm glad you're here, and I hope you come again."

I look around the room, at Anna's hands, resting on her knees; at Caleb's face, his forehead wrinkling but his eyes calm. I think about them looking at me. What do they see?

"As you know, this group isn't about giving advice," Sharon says. "But before we close, I want to share an idea for everyone to think over."

This is different. Sharon's calmness, the way she smiles with her eyes and not only with her mouth, always makes me feel comforted somehow, but she usually doesn't say much. And she *never* tells us what to do.

"This week," she says, "I want you to think of something that's just yours. Something that makes you feel like your worries are slipping away and you're exactly who and where you need to be." She leans forward, her hands clasped over her knees. "Something you can get lost in. And then—" She takes time to let her eyes swoop around the room, locking in on each of us. "Then, I want you to do that thing."

Everyone looks at her, even Anna, who's been staring at the floor ever since she shared.

"Want to know what my thing is?" Sharon asks, her voice low, eyebrows raised, a smile glimmering like she's sharing a secret. "Swimming. I get in the pool, start churning out laps, and all those thoughts weighing me down, they just leave."

"You swim every day?" Caleb's shocked voice breaks the stillness in the room. "Like, all year?"

Sharon laughs. "You bet! And early too. My friends can't believe when I set my alarm." She cups her mouth with both hands and whispers: "Four forty-five a.m. One hundred percent worth it."

I've been to the Belding pool before: cold chlorine, echoes splashing off tile walls. I would usually rather go to Pine Lake and wade in the shallows, over stones, but I can picture Sharon slicing through cool blue, her arms pulling a path to follow, and I can see how it works.

"The more time you can find for your 'thing,'" Sharon says, "the more you'll feel like yourself. And the more you can do that, the more you'll know that your *self* is a pretty great thing to be."

I don't really understand why Sharon's talking about *us*. Aren't we all here because of other people?

In the truck on the way home, I pull Andy's letter out of my pocket and keep reading.

I'M LEARNING A LOT HERE, WHICH IS COOL. A TRACTOR WE USE FOR A LOT OF STUFF AROUND THE FARM BROKE, AND BEN, ONE OF THE STAFF, SHOWED

ME HOW TO FIX IT. YOU KNOW I'VE ALWAYS LIKED CARS,
BUT WOW—THAT FEELING OF WORKING ON SUCH A HUGE
VEHICLE WAS AWESOME. THIS WILL SOUND WEIRD, BUT IT
MADE SENSE RIGHT AWAY, WHAT I WAS SUPPOSED TO DO.
I GUESS IT JUST CAME NATURAL. AFTER I FINISHED, I
KIND OF WISHED THERE WAS ANOTHER PROBLEM WITH
IT, BECAUSE I WANTED TO WORK ON IT ALL DAY! BEN
SAYS IF I LIKE FIXING TRACTORS SO MUCH I COULD
THINK ABOUT BECOMING AN AGRICULTURAL MECHANIC,
AND REPAIRING FARM EQUIPMENT COULD BE MY JOB.
WOULDN'T THAT BE COOL?

BOTTOM LINE, LITTLE C., I FEEL LIKE I'M FINALLY
FIGURING OUT WHO I AM.

I HOPE YOU'RE DOING SOME COOL STUFF TOO. I BET
YOU'RE STAYING BUSY, NOW THAT I'M OUT OF YOUR WAY!

Out of my way? He knows that's not how I feel.
I reread the letter. Andy sounds happy, but I'm also
confused. How can he not know who he is? *I* know
who he is. I've known forever. There's nothing
wrong with fixing tractors, but what else about
him might change while he's gone?

I'm staring out the window, trying to imagine Andy under a tractor, spinning wrenches and screwdrivers, when I remember I didn't look for the punch line about walls. I turn the letter upside down and see one line at the bottom:

I'll meet you at the corner.

The words swim together and I blink hard. Andy can't meet me anywhere. Not now. Even his words make it feel like he's stepping away. And Sharon says I have to find something that's mine. But the things I love most have always been Andy's too.

Suddenly, trees surge in my mind, framed by leaves the colors of fire, hoofprints I can't quite trace, and a jet-black mane that can't be real. Or can it?

CHAPTER 6

"So how much have you figured out about Edna Beard?" I ask. Maya came over to work on our projects, but we decided to start with barn chores. "I mean, that you didn't know before."

"I was googling her again last night. Good old Edna." Maya pushes the door open and flicks on the light. I can already hear Sunny's and Sam's hooves shuffling sawdust. But before we head into the stable, I need to throw down two bales of hay from our loft. Mom and Dad usually move the heavy bales for me, but they must have forgotten.

Maya and I will be able to manage enough to feed Sunny and Sam for now.

I'm not surprised Maya's on a first-name basis with her research subject. They probably would have been great friends in real life; I could see them both burying their noses in crackly newspapers, looking for injustice to fight. "It took some digging, but I found this radio interview with one of her nieces! Primary source!" Maya pumps a fist in the air and I smile. She gets really into school projects, and it helps me get a little more into them too. "Anyway, the niece said Edna was a horsewoman. Isn't that cool?"

"Definitely," I say.

Maya and I start climbing the ladder to the hayloft. I shimmy up fast, skipping rungs. Maya's not as quick, but she makes it up.

"I knew you'd appreciate it," she says, stepping off the last rung and following me to the stack of hay bales. We each grasp one of the two strings that bind the hay together and lug it across the loft, then push it to the ground below. From there, we'll carry flakes into the stable. "Just another reason Edna rules."

"Have you talked about her with your dad?" I ask. Mr. Gonzalez would definitely be proud of Maya for researching Vermont's first female lawmaker. His grandfather, who lived in Mexico, was a judge too, and Maya says that's what inspired him to become one. She's told me stories about meeting her great-grandfather before he died, when her family took a trip back to visit. He only spoke Spanish, but Maya's bilingual, so she could talk to him. I wish I knew a different language. If I had more words to help my ideas make sense, maybe I'd feel brave enough to share them.

Now, Maya looks at the floor and kicks a few stray stalks of hay. "Papi's been kind of out of it lately," she says. Then she turns away and sits on a bale, lying back against a second one and draping an arm across her forehead. I don't know exactly what she means by "out of it," but the dip in her voice makes me not want to ask. "I'm going to wait a little before I tell him about Edna Beard."

I've heard Mr. Gonzalez say that even though we live in a rural area, without all the traffic and people of a city, being a judge is a hard job. "Small town, big problems," he used to tell us, a smile twisting on his face like it was a joke but his eyes sharp and sad. I've known Mr. Gonzalez forever and I like him. He takes Maya and me for ice cream in the summer if we're hanging out near his office in Belding, but he usually walks around with his eyebrows wrinkling together and his phone near his ear or edging out of his pocket.

"I could never, ever be a judge." I shudder. Making decisions for so many people who might have done something wrong, or might not have, would bring the sparrows swooping down for sure.

"Papi says it's really important work." Maya sighs and sits down on a hay bale. "Lately he's been saying that more. He's had some really tough cases and he doesn't have much time to talk." She frowns, and I see her eyebrows wrinkle together for a second, just like Mr. Gonzalez's.

I think then that maybe Maya knows a little bit what it's like for me with Andy. He and I can communicate, but never at the same time. We have to wait between letters just like she has to wait for the right time to talk.

"Hey," Maya says softly, like she can read my mind, "have you heard from Andy lately?"

Maya's brother, Nicolás, is so little, only in second grade, so sometimes I think she must wonder how Andy could end up at the Starshine Center. She picks good times to ask about him, though. Times when she knows the calm inside me wells up thicker than worry.

"I just got a letter today." I reach toward my back pocket, where another envelope waits.

The letter's dated Wednesday, so he must have written it in response to what I mailed on Saturday. I haven't decided how to respond to the one I got earlier this week, about the tractor, but maybe this will give me some hints. I pull it out carefully so I can read parts for Maya. She's the only one besides me who gets to hear Andy's letters.

"DEAR CLAIRE,

HOW DOES THE OCEAN SAY HELLO?"

Maya laughs. "I've only seen it once, when we went to Maine last year," she says. "But okay, I'll think about it." She usually figures out Andy's punch lines before I do.

I read the first part, about how he went on a group hike the day before and made it all the way up Mount Chicory.

"I KEPT FALLING BEHIND EVERYONE ELSE BECAUSE I COULDN'T STOP LOOKING AROUND. SERIOUSLY, IF YOU'D BEEN THERE, YOU'D UNDERSTAND! I KEPT STARING OUT AT THESE TREES—THE COLORS ARE AWESOME RIGHT NOW, JUST LIKE THEY MUST BE AT HOME—AND I'D START THINKING ABOUT HOW ALL THE LEAVES WERE WAVING AROUND LIKE HANDS BECAUSE IT WAS WINDY. DAMIAN AND MARIE KEPT YELLING MY NAME TO GET ME BACK ON TRACK."

Maya rolls her eyes. "Classic," she says.

"Yeah." I laugh. "Spacing out and thinking leaves are hands? Sounds about right."

But I love whenever Andy sees the woods that way and tells me about it. He's the reason I grew up looking at everything a little longer, a little closer.

"So, Damian and Marie," Maya says. "Does he talk about them a lot?"

"He's started to." I chew my lip, trying to picture what Damian and Marie look like. To me they seem murky, just barely real. But Andy sees them every day. I shiver, look back down at the letter, and keep reading.

"It reminded me of Pebble Mountain, because you could see forever up there. Remember how I used to tell you if Pebble Mountain were a little taller, we could reach up and grab stars to put in our pockets? You believed it. You were pretty little then. But honestly, I kinda believed it too. Anyway, I guess Mount Chicory's even bigger! Elizabeth—that's one of our therapists—said it was a good way to get perspective, and I was thinking about that. Like what kind of perspective I might need. Before Starshine, everything I did felt really big. It mattered so much. On Mount Chicory, I felt small. But kind of in a good way. Does that make sense?"

Maya nods slowly. "He's deep. I think I get it, though?"

I know exactly what he means. "It's like that in the woods too. When I'm riding Sam, and all I see around me are trees, I kind of blend in. I'm still a part of things, just not a major part."

It feels good to be tucked in with something bigger, something strong and growing and real that won't flutter away.

"So you asked if I was homesick. Tough question, Little C."

"Seriously?" Maya asks, grimacing. "I'd definitely be homesick."

A sparrow pokes its beak at my heart, and I feel it like a pinprick, tiny but sharp.

"Everything's all planned out here. To the point where it's kind of like, all I have to do is think. Figure things out, like I told you about with the tractor. It's been kinda cool."

I don't know why Andy couldn't think at home, though. We always said we did our best thinking up on Pebble Mountain, under the big quiet of stars and pine cones and skies first washed with sunset oranges and pinks, then purpling to black.

Maya looks at me, tips her head to one side. "He didn't say he *never* wants to come home."

"I know." But my voice feels thick and heavy. "And further down he says he misses me. He always says that."

I don't read that part aloud. But I have it memorized: DON'T WORRY ABOUT ME, LITTLE C. YOU SOUNDED WORRIED IN YOUR LAST LETTER. BUT I'M OKAY. AND I'LL BE EVEN BETTER. I'VE ALREADY GOTTEN STARTED.

I didn't think I wanted him to be better. I just wanted him to be *him*.

"Oh, I got it!" Maya says suddenly. "It's like the trees. It waves."

"What?" I swipe a palm across my eyes, start folding the letter.

"You forgot to read the end of the joke. But I already know it." Maya points to the letter, and I open it back up. She's right: IT WAVES. "That's the thing I remember most about the ocean. Papi wanted to go fishing, but the waves were so big we had to turn around."

Maya looks down at her knees, picks wisps of hay out of her shoelaces. Her voice dropped low again.

"Hey," I say, "let's throw down another bale and get going with chores. That way we can get back to my house and talk more about your project." If Maya's dad can't give her the time right now, at least I can.

I walk back over to the stack of bales, but my mind is full of everything else: Maya's quietness, Andy's strange words, the horses—

Suddenly, my boot catches and I come down hard, my palms slamming the floor.

"*Ow!*" I yell. I rub my knees, which I can tell are scraped underneath my jeans, then look back to figure out why I fell.

"Are you okay?" Maya leans over, pulls me up.

I never noticed that crooked old sticking-up

floorboard before, but now I have to wrestle it up a little bit before banging it back into place. When I do, something gleams underneath, and I feel my fingers clamping onto the edge of a box.

It's an old box, banged up and bent, the color of bridle buckles. It isn't heavy, but it feels important, like the thunder that comes rippling over the mountains just before a storm.

The box is quieter than that, but it surprises me just the same. The air around it shimmers.

My mind races. A long time ago, when my grandparents had dairy cows, they kept the hayloft in good repair. The chances the same floorboard was loose back then are pretty slim. I could be the first person to find this box in a while, maybe ever.

I slip the box out and shake it, hear a rattling. It has a little lock, the kind that hooks around a latch. A tiny keyhole. I swish loose hay around on the floor a little bit, run my hands over the rough grain of the wood, and look for a key. Nothing.

"I'm going to need a bolt cutter," I say. And then I realize how much I want Andy here, how much I need him to go right to the spot on the barn wall where we hang tools and grab the bolt cutter without even needing to look because he knows exactly where it hangs and how it feels, the rubber handles curving away from a biting metal mouth.

"Tell me what it looks like," Maya says, already stepping carefully onto the ladder and lowering herself down, rung by rung.

"Red handles!" I call.

When she comes back up, I take the bolt cutter quickly and touch the box again.

But then I wait another moment. I have this feeling that's hard to describe. When I was ten and showed Sam at the fair for the first time, in the Western Pleasure class, I remember looking up at the people sitting all around. Some of them were taking swigs of soda or checking their phones or leaning in to say something about the horses or the weather, but a lot of them were looking right at me and my skinny birch-bark arms holding the reins strong because I know just how to do it, and I realized: *These are the last thirty seconds of me being the person I've been.* I knew that when I signaled, Sam would bring me into the ring with every muscle pulling hard under his soft coat and I would be different. For a moment, everything and everyone in the ring, even me, froze. Then I squeezed my legs against his sides and told my old self goodbye.

Now I feel like it's time to do that again.

I put both my hands on the sides of the box's top and push in a little, then lift. The metal catches at the corner and I have to jimmy it around and use one hand to hold the bottom down hard and the other to push the lid up, and it opens.

I guess in the couple of minutes that passed between finding the box and opening it, I must have been expecting to find a pile of gold coins or a winning lottery ticket or something like that. I know I wasn't expecting what I *do* find, which seems pretty ordinary. There are two bits that I know must have been shiny once but have gone dull and gray after resting in horses' mouths for however long, years probably. There's a scrap of leather curled into itself, kind of ripped on two ends and cracked, maybe a foot long. There's a stone, big enough to feel heavy in my palm and beautiful too, black but with little bits of silver laced all through. I've never seen one quite like it, not in our woods on Pebble Mountain where I climb on big boulders, and not on either of our beaches where I dig into the sand and fill my pockets with freshwater mussel shells.

Maya leans over my shoulder and shrugs. "Some box," she says. "What is all that anyway?" She presses her hands to her knees and stands up.

"Looks like horse stuff," I say. "This piece of leather probably came from some kind of harness. See the holes in it?"

At first I think that's it. Two bits, a scrap of leather, and a stone.

But at the bottom there's one more thing. I probably didn't see it at first because it was flat and about the same size as the box, but I realize it's an envelope, and I work my fingers around it to get it out.

I have to be careful because it's a little stuck to the bottom of the box, like it's been there a long time, and the envelope is so old and yellowy white that it feels like it might disintegrate. I work it out and turn it over in my hands. It must have been so long since someone put it there that it isn't even sealed anymore: The top flap kind of pops open.

From inside the envelope I pull out a piece of newsprint. "Cool," I say. "Maya, look, this is from the *Tribune* and it's super-old—it says March 9, 1925."

Maya squats back down on her heels and leans forward a little bit. Then she sucks her breath in when I read the headline aloud: *"Pebble County Boy, 12, Survives Fall."*

In the picture under the headline, a boy stares at me with hollow eyes.

Maya leans in closer. "What does it say?"

I scramble to my feet. "I'll read it to you."

"Twelve-year-old Jack Hamilton is now recovering at home after an overnight hospital stay during which he received treatment for hypothermia.

In the late afternoon of March 7, 1925, Hamilton had driven his family's team of horses onto frozen Cedar Lake, apparently as a shortcut home from bringing a load of empty sap buckets to his cousin. Warm daytime temperatures over the past week made for productive sugaring but weakened the ice, and the horses fell through.

Hamilton managed to exit the sinking wagon and, half-submerged, leveraged himself onto the surface when his wet sleeve made contact with the ice and froze there. He was soon noticed by Lester Annis, a neighbor driving by, and rescued when Annis ventured onto the ice with a rope and pulled him in.

The horses and wagon were lost."

Maya and I don't say anything at first. We don't even look at each other. I hold the paper in my hands and watch the boy's sad eyes as if I expect them to blink.

"Have you ever heard that story before?" I ask. Maya shakes her head.

Neither have I, but I can't shake the feeling that burns through my fingers when I touch the cool metal. I just *know* there's something about that box. How did it end up in *our* barn? For the first time, I wonder who might have lived here before my great-grandparents. Was it this boy?

And then my mind fills with snow-dusted trees, a flowing black tail. Jack's story seemed to end differently than anyone would have expected. A miracle—exactly like what I think I saw in the woods. I wonder—but then I shake my head. Then wonder again.

One thing about horses is they rely on instinct. They can't explain to you why sometimes they stop right where they are and point their ears forward so hard that the veins under the skin bulge and their nostrils widen and flare and their feet dig into the ground like posts. Andy always says people can't know the half of what horses smell on the wind or hear in the brush. There's a whole world they experience that we can only guess at.

Deep down, I know that the box is part of that world and I need to pay attention to it.

CHAPTER 7

"Okay." I take a deep breath and clench the sides of the box. "I have to tell you something. This box is super-random, but it's not the only strange thing I've seen lately." I'm a little nervous to tell Maya about the woods, but at the same time, I *have* to. Maya and I don't keep secrets from each other.

"I can handle 'random,'" Maya says. "What's going on?"

I describe the mysterious dappled horse in the woods, the one Sunny and Sam also seemed to see.

"Are you serious?" Maya asks, her eyes wide. "That's...honestly, very weird."

"I know," I say. "But seeing that horse, or parts of it, I guess—it was really good at hiding—and then finding this box...it feels important somehow. Like maybe they're connected."

"Well, we're obviously going to have to look for this random forest horse," Maya says. "Like, now."

"Now?" For once, I'm not sure I want to go back into the woods. I feel like I need to be more prepared or something.

"Definitely now," Maya says. "What's the point of waiting? If we see it again, we'll know there's really something there, and we can figure out how to deal with it."

Whenever I can't decide what to do, Maya can. And she's usually right. "Well...we can't take the horses," I say. "I would get in so much trouble."

"So let's walk." Maya's voice sounds like itself again, full of music and just on the edge of laughing. That makes me want to stick with her plan even though I have no idea how long it will take us to walk to where I saw signs of the horse before.

I check my watch: 5:35 p.m. We still have half an hour before I need to be back for dinner, and before Maya's mom picks her up. "Okay," I say. "Let's see how far we can get."

Leaves crunch under our boots, and Maya shuffles her toes forward and to the side, tossing some in my direction. I kick a few back at her.

"Oh, no you don't," she says, bending down and scooping a huge pile.

"You started it!" I shriek just as she hurls the entire armful at my face. I blink and laugh, damp earthy smells filling my nose as I grab my own leaves and throw them back.

We're both laughing, wiping itchy stems off our necks, when I remember my watch hands moving.

"Let's go." I jog the rest of the way to the woods, and Maya matches my pace.

Stepping past the threshold between field and forest feels like walking into a church full of stained-glass windows, only the windows are the trees: maples burning red and orange, yellow aspen shivering, and cedars a velvety green. I want to close my eyes and feel the hushed air drifting through bony branches, but I want to keep them open too and see everything.

The trees make me think again about the wisp of tail I saw last time I went into the forest. Hooves, pounding. Ripples of muscle, shining. I'm glad I told Maya about it. I want to tell Andy too, but his letter about liking Starshine Center makes me wonder if he'd want to know, if he still thinks about home as much as I think of him.

From hidden places come the sparrows, fluttering in my chest, and the spinning and whirling I always feel when I'm not sure how something I'm about to do will turn out. But this time the feeling makes me want to go faster. The sparrows never stay long when I'm in the woods.

Ten more minutes in, when Maya and I are both breathing hard and I can feel blood pulsing in my skull, I slow down. The forest has grown perfectly still, but it hums too. We haven't gone as far as Mom and I did, but the shimmering air makes me think we're getting close. I start taking more careful steps, then stop and lean against a towering spruce, letting my head rest on its scratchy trunk.

Maya stands next to me and looks into the sky. We both stay perfectly still and listen.

At first there aren't any sounds. I don't expect too many birds to be singing in fall, but I don't even hear leaves rustling.

Then, a nudge at my elbow. Soft breath just below my shoulder.

I spin back and a quick thunder pounds away past the spruce, dappled haunches blending into the colors all around. I suck in a quick breath, follow the sound.

I look at Maya, my eyes wide.

She shakes her head, lifts her shoulders in a confused shrug.

I whip my head back around just in time to see a new set of silvery-gray legs lifting away, different hooves kicking up leaves, another black mane streaming past the trees.

A high-pitched peal rings through the air, like the sound of a bell but harsher. Not the trill of a wood thrush, not the tiny shriek of a mouse being caught and pierced, but something fuller. The call of a horse. It's gone before I've fully realized what it is, and I look up, trying to find where it came from.

Over my head, the sky cracks open and raindrops begin to lightly fall. They make curtains between the trees and suddenly everything hides behind little white stars.

But through the rain, I *see* her. She's standing in a cluster of cedars, her forelock long and curling. Her ears pricked forward. Her eyes muddy brown and gentle.

I take one step toward the horse. I don't know if I can squeeze through the narrow spaces between the trees, but I have to try.

"Stay," I whisper. Her nostrils flare. I hear her breath.

One more step, the crackle of leaves as they give way under my boot. I hold my hand out so she can catch my scent without touching. She jerks her head back, startling.

I stop, take a deep breath in, feel how the calm that always comes when I'm near Sunny and Sam rushes in and blooms through every part of me.

It's okay. The words are clear, but I've just thought them. Sent them her way on a current of air.

We both stand staring, so close that if I reached my arm all the way out and she stretched her neck forward, my fingertips could touch the silver whiskers on her chin. She drops her head, turns enough so I can see the blue and white flecks splattering the darkness of one eye. A moon eye.

Then she spins on her back feet and melts away, leaves and rain dripping from branches to cover her tracks.

Gone.

I can't believe it at first. I can't move. I look at the empty place she left, trying to bring her back there with only my wanting.

But I can feel the distance growing. She's far away now. And overhead, the rain falls faster.

I check my watch: 6:00. Even if we run out of the woods, we'll barely make it back home before Mom tries calling me on her own phone, or worse, puts her coat on, steps into her boots, and comes looking for me.

"There were two," I whisper. "Did you see them?"

"I...don't really know, Claire," Maya says. "I mean, I could tell you were looking really carefully—"

"No." My mind races. I keep seeing the matching silvery coats and charcoal-black manes and tails. "There were definitely two."

"Maybe next time you could get pictures," Maya says.

"I'm worried taking out my phone will startle them, and besides, the camera on this thing stinks," I say. "You know yours does too." But I'm distracted now, worried about time. "We have to go."

Maya nods quickly, like she's coming out of a trance. "I'm right behind you."

Trees spin past as we hurtle down the path, leaves spraying behind us. I'm squinting into cold rain, wiping my eyes so I don't lose the path blurring in front of me.

When we're out of the woods, the rain hits harder on the open path to the barn, and I'm relieved when I reach the front door and can lean over, grabbing my knees and letting my heartbeat slow.

Tires crunch in the driveway, and I look past the barn to see Ms. Gonzalez's car rolling down the lane.

"Wow. Nice timing, Mami," Maya says. She stands up straight, wipes raindrops off her cheeks, and holds up a hand for a high five as she walks toward the car. I follow.

"Hi, girls!" Ms. Gonzalez calls out the window. "How's it going?"

"Good!" I call back. "Maya and I were... researching."

Ms. Gonzalez nods slowly. "In the rain," she says. "Got it. This History Fair project has certainly captured Maya's interest. And yours too, it seems."

You could say that, I think, even though I'm not quite sure yet what the horses in the woods have to do with my project. I only know I need to find them. They remind me of Andy's stars, of his waving leaves, of the way he seems to see everything.

"Claire, tell your mom I'll call her soon," Ms. Gonzalez says. "I'm short on time, or else I'd come in."

"No problem." I watch Maya as she watches me, waving out the rear window as the car moves away. Then I adjust my hat, carefully wipe my hair out of my eyes, take a deep breath, turn to the house, and push our door open.

Dad's car is in the driveway, which means he's probably upstairs changing, maybe lying on his and Mom's bed with his eyes closed for a few minutes, thinking about the students he helped that day and the ones he worries he's not doing enough for. When he comes downstairs, he'll ask how my day was and I'll only know if his was harder or easier by the way his neck either bends forward, like it's being pushed by a heavy weight from behind, or rolls back, relaxed and strong at the same time.

Either way, I expect Mom to be standing in the kitchen doorway with her hands on her hips and her face creased in lines of worry.

But when I open the door, I just hear quiet. I smell chili simmering in the pot on the stove, and the oven light's on, with corn bread baking.

"Mom?" I call. "Dad?"

"In here, Claire!" Mom's voice drifts over from the living room.

She's hunched at her desk, typing on the computer. "Your dad's upstairs," she says. "He'll be down soon. Did you set the table?"

She didn't even realize I was late. Relief mixes with a sharp pang, a feeling I can't quite name. I step far enough behind her to see what's on the screen, and article titles pop out: "Helping Your Child Through Addiction" and "Adolescent Journeys into Recovery" and "A Family Affair: Substance Abuse in Teens."

"What are you reading?" I ask, even though I know now. I pretend to look only at her eyes anyway, so she won't know what I saw over her shoulder.

She tells me the truth, partly. "Just some research."

"June." My dad's voice is soft but heavy at the same time. I turn and see him taking the last step down the stairs. He's wearing sweatpants and the old scratchy sweater Gram knit him before she died. When he runs one hand through his hair, making it stick up at the ends, I can tell it's been one of his harder days. "Let's take a break."

"But I—" Mom shakes her head.

"I know you're trying to help," Dad says, his hands on her shoulders. "But it also stresses you out. Plus, Andy's already getting help. That's the point."

Then he turns to me. "Hey, kiddo. Your cheeks are so red. Were you running or something?"

Mom looks at me like she's seeing me for the first time. "Claire was doing chores," she says. "Right?" I can tell she's not so sure anymore.

"Yeah," I say. "Just chores." But I can feel my face flushing even redder. "I'm going to go set the table. Oh, by the way, Mom—Ms. Gonzalez says she'll call you soon."

"I've been meaning to talk to her," Mom says. "Thanks for the reminder."

As I lay out bowls and spoons, sour cream and cheese for the chili, and butter and jam for the corn bread, I feel my fingers itch, wanting to write

Andy another letter. I already know how it will start:

> Dear Andy,
>   Guess what? There are wild horses living in the woods.

Maybe if Andy sees that home isn't only what he remembers, if he also knows it's full of secrets he's never seen, he'll want to come back.

CHAPTER 8

When I come in from the barn late Saturday morning, Mom's left a note on the kitchen table: *Went grocery shopping. See you at lunch!*

Dad's gone too, distributing pizzas for a high school fundraiser. That means I have the house to myself, at least for now.

The silence feels a little strange, but peaceful.

I'm about to grab my latest letter to Andy from my desk and walk to the mailbox when I hear the door open.

It can't be Mom or Dad; they'd be talking to each

other and yelling hello to me. My throat tightens, but when I go to the door I can see it's just Nate, Andy's friend from school. We've known Nate for a long time, and he's used to walking right in. But he hasn't come around since a while before Andy left. Now, he has one foot in the house, one still on the front stoop.

"Hey, Nate," I say. "Come on in."

"Claire!" Nate says. He hesitates, then steps the rest of the way inside, letting the door shut behind him. "I didn't know anybody was home." He looks tired, his blue eyes bleary.

"Oh, um—okay," I say. "Did you need something? You know Andy's not—"

"At home. Yeah, I know." Nate stuffs his hands in his pockets, looks down at his feet. "I was actually coming by because I left something in his room. I thought maybe I could get it."

It's weird that Nate just walked right in. That he isn't even looking at me. He glances to one side, then the other. "Um…" I chew my lip.

"It's just—it's this textbook?" He's talking a little too fast. "I brought it over before Andy left. I was showing him all the stuff for my community college classes."

"So an economics book?" I remember Nate saying that's what he was going to study after graduation. But haven't classes already started? Wouldn't Nate have needed the book weeks ago?

"Well..." He looks past my shoulder. "I'll definitely know it when I see it. Maybe I can go take a look?"

I remember Nate showing me how to put Legos together when he was in sixth grade and I was in kindergarten. He and Andy used to tell knock-knock jokes that left me laughing so hard my stomach hurt. But now sparrows whir above my head.

"I guess so," I say, even though flutters fill my chest. *It's just Nate*, I tell myself. "My parents will be back soon. You could have lunch with us."

Nate backs toward the door, pushes it open. "Oh, actually, yeah, you know what? No worries. I can come some other time."

He waves and starts jogging toward his truck.

"Can you at least tell me the book title?" I call. "I can let you know if I find it."

Nate revs the engine. "Nah, you don't have to look!" he yells over the growl. "See you around!" The tires screech a little as he peels away. The sparrows still quiver, Nate's words caught in their wings.

As soon as the sound of the truck fades, I move from the porch back into the house and start up the stairs. When I reach the closed door of Andy's room, I stop, my hand on the knob.

Then I twist it open and tiptoe in.

The whole room holds its breath. It's exactly like he left it. His bed in the corner, the blue comforter on top. His desk with the coffee mug full of pens. His backpack, still full of senior-year binders. On the ceiling: those glow-in-the-dark stars, arranged in perfect constellations.

I touch the comforter on his bed. Pull open his desk drawer. Run my finger along the top of his bookcase, where model cars and graphic novels and speakers line the shelves.

No textbook.

I slip into his closet. It's long and narrow, the ceiling sloping down at the far end to make a sharp angle with the floor. Andy never really kept much in there, just piles of extra bedding and off-season clothes. It's pretty hard to crouch down far enough to get to the back anyway. But when we were younger, we used to drape his comforter over the rack where he hung shirts and pants, making a kind of curtained fort. He'd light a flashlight and tell me ghost stories.

One tug, and the comforter's hanging in the closet again. I'm way too big for this, but I crouch behind it anyway and try to imagine Andy's voice, how it sounded when he was my age.

And then I remember the Secret Pillow.

The Secret Pillow looks normal from the outside, but under the plaid flannel case there's a slit in one side that Andy and I used to stuff things inside. Jolly Ranchers, Lego creations, tiny cars, packs of gum, notes. We stopped using it once Andy got into high school. I don't even know if he still has it.

But when I dig past folded quilts, I find it's still there after all, nestled with other spare pillows we barely use. I'm not expecting to find a textbook when I reach deep into it, but I'm not expecting what I do find either, which is a bag of something plastic and rattling. Containers of pills.

These must be the pills that Andy took. Why are there so many? Maybe he was saving a lot for later. But then, how did he get them? I riffle through the pillow, not sure what I'm looking for, when my hand brushes against something else. It's a cell phone, one of those ancient ones, nothing like the smartphone in Andy's desk drawer. When I press the POWER button, it surprisingly turns on without any trouble, though the battery looks low. The contacts list doesn't have Mom or Dad or me, though. I don't recognize a lot of the names. But I do see Nate's.

I push the bag back into the Secret Pillow and shove it under Andy's quilts, my heart pounding so hard it feels like it's outside of me somehow.

With shaking fingers, I put the comforter back on the bed. Then I tiptoe out of the room, just like I tiptoed in. I shut the door so quietly I barely hear the latch click into place.

All I can think is that I have to mail Andy's

letter. I still remember what I wrote at the end, after telling him about the wild horses:

> It probably sounds strange.
> But you know how you told me we
> could grab stars to keep in our pockets?
> We were younger then and maybe
> you didn't mean it, but still, you showed
> me how to notice things more. And if
> you had been in the woods with us,
> believe me, you would have noticed this!
> I can't wait to show you.
> Come home!
>
> Love,
> Claire

I seal the letter and put a stamp in the corner of the envelope. Outside my window, I almost think I can hear the hooves pounding. I'm itching to go back into the woods, but it takes a while to hike as far as Maya and I did the other day. I have another idea.

Then the front door opens and I hear Mom's

and Dad's voices murmuring. Walking downstairs, I work through a plan in my mind.

Dad's already pulling sandwich fixings out of the refrigerator. "Hungry?" he asks.

I nod and start pouring water into glasses. I lift one, take a long drink. With every swallow, I bury the knowledge of what I saw in Andy's closet so deep inside I don't know if I'll find it again.

By the time I speak, my voice matches my insides: steady and calm.

"You know Sharon, our group facilitator?" I put my sandwich together and look up just enough to watch Mom and Dad trying not to act surprised that I'm talking about the support group at all.

"Of course," Dad says, coughing into his elbow. "Sharon."

Mom's eyes flit to Dad's, then back again. "What about her, honey?" Mom's trying not to sound too eager, but it doesn't work.

"In our last meeting she told us all to find something we really loved to do," I say. "Something we can do *by ourselves*." I swallow hard and feel the weight of those last two words. "I guess it's sup-posed to help us feel...better about stuff."

"I can see the value of that," Mom says.

Dad nods. He looks quickly at Mom, then back at me. "Did you have any ideas about what would work for you?" he asks.

"I really want to go riding in the woods more," I say. "By myself."

Mom's eyes get full-moon big.

"I have a phone," I say. "And I'll stay in our woods, on the trails. I won't go past them onto the state land."

Dad steeples his hands, looks at Mom. "What are you thinking, June?"

Mom takes a deep breath. Her eyes are full of questions she's not asking. *Why don't you want to go together? Why do you want to start riding on your own now, when we can't keep the horses for much longer? What are you looking for?*

"I...suppose it could work," she says slowly. "But there would have to be some very clear rules."

I'm too excited to care what rules Mom comes

up with, and I clasp my hands together under the table to keep from bursting out of my chair.

"Your helmet at all times, of course. You'd have to actually bring your phone *and* have it on," Mom says. "It's no use if it's sitting here on the counter, or on silent. And *only* stick to the paths. No bushwhacking."

"I know." I've always seen the wild horses from the path anyway.

"You know the weather can be unpredictable, especially later in October," Mom adds. "No riding if we've had any freezing rain, or—I hate to say this when it's technically still fall, but we all know it could happen—snow."

"But—" I start, then shut my mouth. "Okay."

I definitely don't want to screw this up. Being able to go into the woods alone with Sam will give me exactly what I need: proof of something new, to draw Andy back and make him excited about coming home.

"Text us when you leave," Mom continues. "Then again when you get back. I don't want to have to wonder if you're just taking your time in the barn or getting lost in the woods. And don't stay out longer than an hour."

I silently thank Sharon for giving Mom a reason to say yes in the first place. Who knows how much ground Sam and I will be able to cover in an hour, but it will be a lot more than Maya and I did.

"Thanks, Mom!" Without really thinking, I jump up and wrap my arms around her neck. She squeezes me once, then twice, like she used to when I was little. *One squeeze for love, and one for good luck.* It feels good to hug Mom like that again.

"Thank your father too," Mom says. "You know he worries."

Furrows run across Dad's forehead like the little rivers around his tired eyes. But he smiles at me, and I give him a high five. High fives are our thing.

"Does this count as me texting you?" I ask. "I'm going to head out to the barn now."

But Mom shakes her head. "Nope. Text right before you leave. That way I know how to time the hour accurately," she says. "And when to worry."

"You won't have to worry," I call over my shoulder. I'm already at the front porch, pulling my barn boots over my jeans.

Mom's extra squeeze worked, because it's a perfect day to ride: the sky robin's-egg blue, the leaves bright as paint splotches against it.

I don't take my time grooming Sam. "Guess what!" I tell him. "We're going out all by ourselves today. Can you believe it?"

Sam blows softly through his nose. He's always calm enough for both of us. When I climb onto his back, the memory of the pills in the closet slips away, dissolves under the leaves far below.

But even Sam seems surprised as we start toward the woods. He picks his feet up a little higher than usual, his back muscles quivering. Maybe it's the way I'm holding the reins tighter than Mom would want me to. I feel my thighs tingle as I press them to Sam's sides, and Mom always says horses sense even the smallest changes in their riders' bodies.

"What do you think, buddy?" I ask. "How many will we find today?"

It doesn't take long for Sam to answer. At the exact point where the trail splits—one path looping and curving east through our woods and the other pointing toward the state land bordering Pine Lake—he quickens his pace north even though we usually stick to the circles among the trees we know.

I realize I'm not exactly steering him, not giving him the kinds of strong signals Mom says horses need. *This must be the right direction*, I think. *The way we're meant to go.*

A sound gathers behind us, a heaviness pulsing on frozen ground. Sam slows, and I turn just in time to see two horses—they must be the same ones I saw when I was with Maya the other day—moving through and around trees. They still seem only half real, the foggy color of their bodies blending in with birch bark, maple leaves, and crooked branches. But they gain ground and move in front of us, their dark tails flashing, so I nudge Sam into a canter, hoping to keep up.

We're still on a flat, wide path, so Mom wouldn't worry about this. Still, as we follow the hoofprints unfolding ahead of us, the silvery-gray horses just out of sight, I can tell that we're going farther than we have before.

What did Jack Hamilton's horses look like? I wonder. The photo in the newspaper only showed him, his dark eyes piercing the camera.

Those horses died, I remind myself. *And it was so long ago.*

Still, I can't shake the feeling that Jack and his horses are connected to the ones we're following.

Even though I don't know exactly where I am, I can tell we're getting close to water. Through the thick stands of trees, I catch glimpses of rippling blue: Pine Lake.

I've lost track of the horses. They seem to have vanished, swept away like smoke. But the hollows pressed into the messy leaves in front of us still look like hoofprints.

They led us here.

The wide path trickles to an end in the cedars where hoofprints scatter in every direction. Mom's voice swells in my head: "*Only* stick to the paths." But if I do that, I can't follow the hoofprints or find whatever it is I'm looking for.

So I make my own path.

I take a deep breath, then nudge Sam into the narrow openings between trees, slow and careful.

We're close to the fence line separating our land from the state land and the rocky shore of Pine Lake. We shouldn't go much closer; I don't want Sam getting tangled in anything dangerous. For a second, I wonder if I should get off and walk him.

But around a curve ahead, past the fence, there's a cavern that seems to have been scooped out between the lake and the forest floor. I see something: an opening, ringed by stones. Sam and I go just a little farther.

Why do those look so familiar? I peer closely at the stones and at the dark hollow behind them. They look exactly like the stone from the box: deep black, laced with silver. Only here, there are hundreds.

I catch my breath. Until I opened the box, I'd never seen stones quite like this, and I've never seen this cavern when I've been swimming in Pine Lake or even when Andy took me out in the canoe and we paddled all the way around. Was it always here, and I never noticed? Or did it suddenly appear, like the horses in the woods?

I bring Sam a little closer, but there's not much room. On windy days, the waves probably push through the darkness, but the water's still now, and the hollow in the stones leads somewhere I can't see.

"Okay, Sam," I say. "We're out of time. Let's go." As I turn him back around to retrace our steps, I take just one more look past the fence, at the stony cavern that somehow feels more gentle than scary. It's a place I should tell Andy about. A place I want to come back to.

The whole way home, Sam and I ride alone. I look for hoofprints in the leaves, but they're gone.

Still, I can almost hear the stones whispering that I've already found what I need.

CHAPTER 9

At the support group meeting on Monday, I pick a seat next to Nari again.

"Hi," she says this time. I'm surprised—she's usually quiet, which is one reason why I like to sit next to her. Before, she's only ever smiled at me.

But Sharon's making some notes in a little book and checking her watch, which means the meeting hasn't started yet and maybe Nari figures she has extra time.

I feel a light flutter at the base of my throat, but I swallow it down. "Hi," I say.

"I'm Nari." She smiles, tugging at the long black braid hooked over her amber shoulders. I'm trying to figure out what it is about her voice that makes me hope she'll keep talking. It's soft, like falling leaves. But there's something else underneath it that isn't so soft, that might have harder edges. Maple bark. Glittering frost. And that makes me think Nari is strong too.

"I guess you know that, actually." She's laughing now, rolling her eyes. "We say it every week, during introductions. You're Claire."

I laugh too. At first it feels strange to laugh in this room, but then it feels kind of okay. "Yeah, I'm Claire."

Words bubble up inside. Suddenly I want to ask Nari all kinds of things, like who she's here for and why she comes back and if it's helping and even what she might do with pills she found in her brother's Secret Pillow. But then Sharon clears her throat and her silver bracelets jingle as she clasps her hands and tells us it's time to get started.

"Welcome," Sharon says, like we're at a fancy hotel and not a meeting for family members of people who, like Mom would say, "struggle with addiction," and who maybe left, and made a big empty space wherever they used to be. But Sharon says it again: "Welcome. It's good to have you all here."

Sharon holds up a piece of paper. "Our opening reflection today comes from an article called 'What We Can't Control,'" she says. "Would anybody like to read?"

Nari raises her hand. "I will."

Sharon has a bunch of short readings she likes to use. When Dad first brought me to the support group, she encouraged me to borrow some, but I said, "No, thanks." She hasn't asked again.

Nari leans over the paper and takes a deep breath. When she starts reading, her voice is clear and strong.

"Isn't it easy to want to control everything that happens? It seems like if we can only say or do the right things, life will work out the way we hope. But then, what do we do when nothing seems to be going according to plan?"

Nari pauses for a second. Smiles. Then keeps reading.

"It's especially easy for our plans to fall apart where other people are concerned. We want the people we love to behave just so. Maybe we even think it's possible to change how they act, by force of will."

I look over at Anna, biting her nails. Next to her, Caleb jiggles his leg up and down, his hand gripping his knee so tightly it looks like it might hurt. Marcus sits with his chin in his hands, his dark eyes tired.

"Even though our wishes for these people come from a good place—because we care about them and want the best for them—trying to help control their actions ends up being difficult for everyone."

This is the kind of thing I hear from the support group that doesn't make sense. If we aren't trying to help the people we're here for, what's the point of coming?

"The only actions we can possibly control are our own. And we can't find peace until we let go of trying to control someone else."

Nari stops, then puts the paper down.

"Thanks, Nari, for that reading," Sharon says.

"Let's sit with it. Take a moment to think about those words. They aren't easy, are they?"

A couple of chairs down, I hear someone mutter, "Definitely not." Which is exactly what I'm thinking. Doesn't Andy *need* somebody to help him control his actions?

Silence fills the room and I do what Sharon says. I sit with it. The words burrow under my skin and itch.

Then Marcus clears his throat. "I get it, but I don't," he says. "It just seems like if my dad really cared about me at all, he'd stop drinking. Like it wouldn't be that hard. But he hasn't stopped. So then, why *doesn't* he care about me? Like, what am I supposed to do to make that happen?" Anger burns in his voice, and underneath it's like a paper cut: sharp and painful.

Nobody answers. Marcus's questions hang in the air. "My dad always wants to watch the sports channel," he says. "And even though he drinks when he does it, I watch it too. I don't even like football or basketball, even though now I know all the stupid rules because I've watched so many times, waiting for him to talk to me. He can probably tell I don't like the games that much, though. Maybe if I liked them more, he would like *me* more."

I watch Sharon watch Marcus, her eyes full and warm and reaching somehow, like she wants to wrap Marcus in a hug but all she can do is listen for as long as he needs her to.

Marcus shouldn't *have* to like football or basketball. Maybe everyone else is thinking the same thing and filling all the cracks in Marcus's voice, because he shakes his head suddenly and his face, usually still as a pond, pinches and twists. "No," he says. "When I listen to myself say it out loud, I know that can't be it. That's not it at all."

He leans back in his chair, slumped a little, but his eyes have more light in them now.

Sharon waits another beat, but Marcus doesn't say anything else. "Thanks, Marcus," she says, and we all echo her.

Silence again. The clock on the wall ticks, and my heart beats. Words tangle in my chest, too deep for even me to hear. I just know they're there.

"I thought I could change my sister," Nari says.

Her voice, ringing into the room, sounds different than it did when she said hi. It's even more confident. Full of purpose.

"Seriously, I tried everything." Nari looks at the paper, turns it over in her hands. "Tagging along to do the things she liked. Leaving her alone. Writing her notes. Getting mad at her. None of it helped."

Nari looks around the room, her eyes finding Marcus and Caleb and Anna and kids whose names I've forgotten.

"My sister used to be awesome," Nari continues. "Seriously, the coolest. She was super-funny and the only person I wanted to see when I was having a horrible day. She talked me through so much drama with friends, especially when everyone started getting weird in fifth grade—oh my gosh, I can't even tell you."

Nari shakes her head and looks up at the ceiling, her smile stretching wide like thinking about her sister that way makes everything good again.

"I learned to play guitar because of my sister. She's an amazing singer and I thought it would be so cool to perform, like as a duo. A girl band, sort of. I got pretty good. We would practice in her room, with songs she wrote. She wanted to go on the road together, like during summer vacations—I think she almost kind of convinced Mom and Dad to drive our tour bus, and that's impressive, because I have no idea how they'd ever take time off from work."

I imagine Nari and an older sister I've never met hurtling down mountain roads, singing out the windows.

"When she overdosed, I wondered what I could have done differently. Should I have practiced with her more? Or less? Did I care too much about the band, put pressure on her? Did I annoy her? I thought these things all the time. It made me so tired."

Everyone's looking at Nari, but with different expressions: Marcus relieved, Anna nervous, Caleb hopeful.

"Then she had to go to jail." Nari's face tightens, and she squeezes her hands together. "That was hard." Her voice sounds so quiet at first I think she'll stop talking, but then she shares more.

"Afterward my parents spent all this money to ship her off to some horse camp down in Connecticut that's supposed to help, but she had to go by herself, she couldn't even call us, and at that point I guess I kind of realized, yeah, okay, it's not about me. And it's not because of me." Nari lets out a breath and her shoulders relax. Her voice is steady. "She seems to be doing better now, but not because of anything I did. Just like she wasn't doing worse because of anything I did."

Horse camp? Jail?! I try to absorb everything else Nari said, but I'm stuck thinking about what else we might have in common. I feel the heat from the sparrows' fluttering wings rising up the back of my neck and to my forehead.

"Okay, that's all I wanted to say," she says more softly. "For now."

Nari stands up and hands the paper to Sharon. When she turns back to her seat, her eyes look calm and still as bare fields.

"Thanks, Nari," we say.

Usually, when the meeting ends, I run up the

stairs and out the door. But this time, as Sharon closes, I take a deep breath and turn to Nari.

"Hey," I say. "That was cool, what you shared."

"Oh, thanks." She lifts her backpack to her shoulder. "Once I started talking, I couldn't really stop. It was kind of weird."

"It was interesting," I say. "I can't believe your sister had to go to jail."

"I haven't talked to her much about it," Nari says. "I'm not sure I want to."

I decide to change the subject. "I was wondering— what horse camp were you talking about?"

"It's this camp that's specifically for teenagers who've had issues with addiction," she says. "And their whole thing, like their way of dealing with it, has to do with horses. It's called... what's that word that means *horse*, but starts with an *e*?"

"Equine," I say. "It actually came from an older Latin word: *Equus*, which basically means an animal in the horse family." My throat immediately burns. Why did I even say that? Nari won't care.

But she smiles. "It's cool that you know that.

Equus. So yeah, it's equine therapy. That's what they do at the camp."

"How does it help?" I mean, I know how Sunny and Sam help me. I know how I feel when I step into the barn, how the sparrows fly so far away I can't feel them at all. I never thought about how other people could feel that way too.

"Well, I guess Pia—that's my sister—really likes it," Nari says. "They started by having her learn to take care of the horses every day, feeding and brushing and things like that. She learned about riding too. According to my parents, they watch how she interacts with the horses and use that to figure out what's going on and how to help."

"That sounds right," I say. "You can't really hide stuff from a horse. They sense everything."

Nari cocks her head and looks at me. "You know about that, huh?"

"We own two horses." I smile just thinking about Sunny and Sam, how even the way their jaws crunch as they eat hay and grain sounds peaceful.

"Pia loves them so much now, she wants to

have one at home," Nari says. "But we live in town, so that won't work, and boarding them is really expensive. My parents just poured all this money into the camp too—it's totally impossible to think about owning a horse."

"Can I have your number?" I blurt out. But as soon as I've said the words, warm wind rushes to my face. I don't want to scare Nari away. I try to swallow the words back, but instead, more come out. "I could show you our horses."

The wind blows hotter, but Nari doesn't seem to notice. "Hanging out would be fun," she says, pulling out her phone and stilling the air around me. I type my number into the text message she opens, and we record each other as new contacts. "But honestly, between you and me? I'm kind of scared of horses."

"Seriously?" I try not to sound too surprised, but it never occurred to me that horses could be scary.

"They're really...I don't know." Nari looks to the side, then back at me. She shrugs her shoulders. "Big?"

We both start laughing at the same time.

"Saying it out loud sounds weird," she says, smiling. "But they're scary, okay?"

I shake my head. "Sunny and Sam are big, but they aren't scary. If you met them, you'd see."

A new idea starts to sprout inside, just a tiny one, so small I can barely feel its little leaves bursting. By the time Nari waves goodbye as she starts walking downtown while I wait for Dad's truck to curve around the road and stop for me, my idea's a flower, full and sweet.

Equine therapy. Not only is it the perfect addition to my project, since it shows that horses can still be really useful, but it could give my family exactly what we need: Mom and Dad another source of money, Andy a reason to come home, and me my horses.

CHAPTER 10

When Ms. Larkin gives us time to research in class, I know exactly how I'll spend it. I'm so excited to learn more about equine therapy that I have to map out how I'll be able to squeeze everything in: During a fifty-three-minute social studies block, I'll spend exactly seven minutes going over my notes from the day before and eight minutes reading as much as I can about logging with horses, followed by sixteen more about how horses drove Vermont's maple syrup and farming industries up through the early twentieth century. Finally, the last twenty-two minutes will be for learning everything I can about equine therapy. In a few more days, I should be ready to outline my presentation.

Back, Then to the Future. Machines took over so much of what horses used to do, with skidders that pull trees through the woods and logging trucks that carry them down the roads and skinny blue sap lines replacing hooves and harnesses. But a machine can't do equine therapy.

As I'm sitting down to get an early start before the bell rings for class, Ms. Larkin throws her hands above her head and rushes over to me. "Ooh, Claire!" she calls, weaving her way around the tables while kids slide into their chairs. "You'll never guess what I found out."

But I bet I can guess, actually. I already know Ms. Larkin wants us to use at least two primary sources for our project. I didn't tell her about the box, but I did show her the article about Jack Hamilton, which made her think of an old man who lives over by Cedar Lake on the other side of Belding: Ethan Hamilton. Apparently he fixed up a few issues with her house when he used to work as a handyman, and she promised to find out if he and Jack were related.

I brace myself, holding on to my backpack straps as hard as I can, but I have to let go when Ms. Larkin hands me a piece of paper with, sure enough, Ethan Hamilton's name and phone number scrawled on it.

"Thanks," I say, even though I'm not sure I mean it. On the one hand, I definitely want to know more about Jack, and if this person can help me, great. On the other hand, I don't like talking to new people. And I *really* hate talking on the phone. I stuff the paper into my back pocket.

"You won't believe this," Ms. Larkin says. "Jack Hamilton isn't some distant relation. He was Mr. Hamilton's *father*! Which makes Mr. Hamilton the perfect primary source!" She clasps her hands together and bounces a little on her heels. Teachers get excited over the weirdest stuff.

"Did he say he remembered what it was like to work with horses?" I ask. Since Jack used the horses for sugaring, it's likely he used them for other tasks too. Learning more about how people used to *need* horses feels like the only chance

I have to find a way for Mom and Dad to think we need Sunny and Sam too.

But Ms. Larkin wags her finger at me. "Figuring that out is your job," she says. "I promised to make sure they were connected somehow—that was fair—but you need to do the rest. Mr. Hamilton did say he could talk this weekend, by the way. I bet you'll get so much great material!"

"Cool." I try to sound excited. This could work well for my project—a firsthand interview might impress the judges, and winning that money would pay for extra time with Sunny and Sam.

Maya comes in and sets her backpack down in the seat next to me. "Wow," she says, but her voice sounds heavy. "Already working and class hasn't even started. Who *are* you?"

"I figured out a really cool angle for my project," I say. "Equine therapy."

"E-*what*?" Maya asks.

"Basically, it means using horses to help people feel better," I say. "A girl at my support group meeting told me about it."

"Hey, that means you're talking to people at

the meeting!" Maya holds up her hand for a high five. "Or at least one person. It counts."

"I didn't *share*," I say. "I talked to her afterward. About her sister."

"Nice," Maya says. "It's good for you to make some friends there."

My throat tightens. "I don't know if she's my friend. Not yet anyway."

Maya rolls her eyes. "She sounds nice, Claire. Just go with it!"

Heat spreads to my tongue, now thick and dry. Maya's not usually impatient. "I just don't know if she'll want to hang out."

"Of course she'll want to." Maya's face softens. "You might be a weirdo, but you're a pretty awesome weirdo, you know?" She punches me lightly on the arm. "And the equine therapy sounds interesting for your project."

"Hey," I say. "Speaking of projects, have you told your dad about yours yet?"

Maya shakes her head. She opens her mouth, then closes it again, like letting the words out would be too hard.

The bell rings and Ms. Larkin announces that it's time to start working. "Free-choice seating today," she says. "Perch yourselves wherever you'll be most productive." One of her favorite memes—another huge cat sitting in an overstuffed recliner with the words **I take my sitting very seriously** stamped across the front—is projected on the board, alongside guidelines for research: the importance of using precise search terms, characteristics of reliable websites, and databases where we might find more information.

"And one more thing," she says. "I'd like to see you check in with one new person today—someone who hasn't seen your project yet. Tell them what you're working on and learn something from them too."

I hear the sparrows' fluttering wings above me before I feel them swoop inside. But I close my eyes and breathe. Filling my lungs with air seems to push the sparrows away.

When I open my eyes, Jamila's there. "Hey," she says. "How's it going, Claire?" She smiles and sits in the empty chair next to me.

"Okay," I say, trying not to sound nervous. "What's your project about?"

"Took me forever to decide," she says. "But I'm really into fashion and Ms. Larkin said we should research what we're interested in, so I finally decided to just...research it!"

She shows me her tablet, where she's already started a Google Slides presentation: "Do Clothes Make the Woman?"

"Wow, that's cool," I say. Jamila always wears the neatest outfits, with combinations I'd never think of: Today it's a lime-green skirt and black leggings, plus knee-high boots and a dangly silver necklace over her blue shirt.

"Fashion has been used to oppress women a lot," Jamila says. "But I'm looking at how we can use it now to express our true selves."

It turns out that talking with Jamila is really easy—just like talking with Nari was. When I walk over to Maya, who's settled by the window next to Ms. Larkin's shelf of houseplants, I'm fluttering again, but this time with something like excitement.

Maya and I start clicking through sites. But Maya's not spilling random facts about Edna Beard like usual. I poke her shoulder, and she leans against me for a moment before sitting up and tapping away on the tablet. We work with our arms touching so neither of us has to feel alone.

No matter what I google, or how carefully I comb through our town's online newspaper archives that stretch all the way back to the 1800s, I can't find anything about Jack Hamilton aside from a grainy reproduction of the article I already have. And the paper with Ethan Hamilton's number on it feels like a heavy stone in my pocket.

On the bus ride home from school, I lean my forehead against the cool window. The colors are shifting a little now, quieting down. Before too long the tree-covered mountains sliding past my window will turn brown, waiting for snow.

I shiver, thinking about the phone call. What am I supposed to say to Ethan Hamilton anyway? He wasn't alive when his dad was twelve.

I glance over at Maya, who's biting her lip, her hands twisting in her lap.

"Do you want to come over today?" I dig the paper Ms. Larkin gave me out of my pocket. "Come on, I have to call this guy. And I'm almost as excited about that as I am about selling Sunny and Sam."

That makes Maya smile. "Okay, that's a little dramatic," she says. "It's just talking."

"Not all of us love talking," I say. "Hey, I have an idea. You could do the call and pretend to be me!"

Maya shifts in her seat to face me. "Maybe you can put the phone on speaker when you call, and I'll write down everything you should say, like superfast. Then all you'd have to do is read it."

We both know we're joking, but at least Maya's eyes are glittering more now. "I'm in," she says, right as the bus pulls in to my stop.

As soon as we've both hopped off the last step, I automatically head for the mailbox.

"When was the last time you heard from Andy?" Maya asks.

"You saw the letter from last Friday," I say. "Remember? 'How does the ocean say hello?'"

"Oh yeah." Maya laughs. "That was a good one."

"Well, I wrote him Saturday and told him about the horses in the woods. So I'm really hoping he wrote back."

"Do you think he'll believe you?" Maya asks as I pull a letter out of the mailbox and wave it in the air, a smile stretching across my face.

"Of course," I say, but inside, question marks bloom. "I'm going to save this till we get to the barn."

We head in that direction, our footsteps matching.

"So," Maya says. "Tell me more about the meetings. Nari seems nice."

I shrug. "I don't know much about her yet. But yeah, I like her."

"Are they going to make you share eventually?" Maya asks as we walk.

I shake my head. "They're not going to *make* me. They don't do that."

"Well, that's good, right?" Maya looks at me. "All you have to do is listen?"

"Listening's okay," I tell her. "But I feel like I'm supposed to *be* one of them too. That's what still bugs me."

"I mean, I get that in a way," Maya says. She's using her gentle voice, the one that feels like a woodstove fire once it stops crackling and just gives off warmth instead. "But what's wrong with being one of them?"

Maya's right. There's nothing wrong with the other kids. "I don't know, I just don't want to think about our family being...like that."

Maya's eyebrows crinkle. I can taste how sour my words sounded. Voices from the meeting fill my head. Sparrows rustle.

"I didn't really mean it that way," I say, even though Maya hasn't answered at all. "I'm not saying there's something wrong with their families."

"Well, there's something wrong with everyone's family," Maya says, her voice a cloud hanging over mountains now, full of rain. "It's not like anybody's out there being all perfect, Claire."

"I know that." Heat spreads across my face.

"No, you don't," Maya says. The storm cloud's gone, but her voice sounds pinched. "It's kind of like you want to pretend that Andy doesn't even have a problem."

"I know he had a problem." My voice is almost a whisper. "Has one." I don't like thinking about the pill bottles in his closet. I try to ignore the seasick feeling I get inside when I realize I'm hiding knowing about them from Maya. But it's not until Maya's voice swirls into the same space in my head where Nari's and Marcus's and Anna's and Sharon's already live that I realize why the sparrows swoop and dive whenever I think about Andy.

I want to fix what happened to our family.

I just don't know if I can.

We step inside the barn and I slide my finger through the envelope, trying to remind myself that this is the same Andy who told me the myth of Pebble Mountain, that it was formed when a moose desperate to find her lost baby settled down to sleep, and waited so long that soil crept over her and trees grew. He *has* to believe me about the horses.

"DEAR LITTLE C.,

WHAT KIND OF HORSE LIKES TO BE RIDDEN AT NIGHT?"

"Okay, wait, I know the answer," Maya says. "Everyone does. Andy got really lazy with that one. It's—"

"Shhh!" I hold my index finger to my lips. I don't care about the joke right now. I want to read the rest of what Andy says.

"Read it out loud," Maya says.

I shake my head. "I'll give it to you when I'm done."

SPEAKING OF HORSES...SO YOU THINK YOU SAW SOME IN THE WOODS? WOW. HAVE YOU CHECKED AROUND TOWN? IS ANYBODY MISSING A COUPLE?

That's not the point, I think. *These horses can't belong to anyone. They're different. And I don't think I saw them—I know I did!*

IT'S GREAT THAT YOU'RE STAYING BUSY, ESPECIALLY WITH SUNNY AND SAM. THAT'S DEFINITELY RIGHT UP YOUR ALLEY. YOU SHOULD GET ALL THE TIME WITH THEM YOU CAN. ONE THING WE'VE BEEN TALKING ABOUT A LOT IN GROUP IS THAT WE NEED TO FIND WHAT

THEY CALL "HEALTHY OUTLETS." BASICALLY, THINGS WE
CAN DO THAT WE'LL LOVE ENOUGH TO STAY AWAY FROM
THE BAD STUFF.

That reminds me of what Sharon said, and it's weird to think that Andy and I are hearing similar things in our groups. Isn't *Andy* the one who needs help?

THEY HAD US MAKE LISTS AND IT'S KIND OF FUNNY
WHAT PEOPLE PICK. DAMIAN REALLY LIKES PAINTING
AND HE'S GOING TO TAKE LESSONS AND FOCUS MORE
ON THAT. MARIE IS APPARENTLY A RUNNER, WHICH
SOUNDS LIKE TORTURE TO ME BUT IT WORKS FOR HER.
MY POINT IS, EVERYONE'S DIFFERENT. BUT I'LL AT
LEAST COME ON A RIDE WITH YOU WHEN I GET BACK,
WHETHER WE SEE THOSE MYSTERIOUS HORSES OR NOT.
NOT SURE HOW MUCH TIME I'LL HAVE, BECAUSE I
NEED TO LOOK AT ENROLLING IN SCHOOL TO GET MY
AGRICULTURAL MECHANIC'S LICENSE AND FIND A JOB
AND AN APARTMENT TOO. ELIZABETH AND BEN HAVE
BEEN HELPING ME FIGURE ALL THAT OUT. YOU SHOULD

KEEP DOING YOUR THING EITHER WAY, LITTLE C. YOU'VE
GOTTA STICK WITH WHAT YOU'RE INTERESTED IN.

I fold the letter and frown.

"Hey," Maya says. "You told me I could read it."

"He didn't really say anything." I stuff the letter into my coat pocket.

"You're a bad liar," Maya says. "But no worries—I don't need to read your private stuff. Did you get the punch line, though?"

"I forgot to look." I don't feel like taking the letter back out.

"Nightmare," Maya says. "It's a classic. *Mare*, like a female horse? Get it?"

I laugh weakly. "Yeah, okay."

But all I can think about is the rest of the letter. In between the joke and the promise to ride was the truth: Andy doesn't believe me.

CHAPTER 11

try to push Andy out of my mind, shift my focus to Ethan Hamilton.

"Okay," I say. "I'm going to call him."

Maya smiles. "Want to practice first?"

Sparrows are already soaring down from the rafters of the barn. "I wrote a few notes at school. I think I'd better just do it."

I move to the corner of the hayloft. The box is still there, hidden under a little mound of hay I scooped over it, and my heart starts knocking against my ribs. I peek inside and everything's exactly as I left it: the bits, the harness, the stone.

And the article. I lift it out and it shakes a little in my hands.

The sparrows swoop down through my throat and up to my head, then tumble into one another. I squeeze my eyes shut tight. The flutter feeling isn't supposed to happen here. The barn is my safe place, with nobody but me and the people and animals I trust. This is definitely the best place to make a phone call to some stranger.

But that doesn't mean I'm not nervous.

I look at Jack Hamilton's eyes, staring out at me from nearly a century ago. I rest my hands against my belly button and breathe in. Then out. Then in again. And out again.

Jack's eyes stay the same. They watch as the sparrows inside me blink and quiet and disappear.

I press SEND.

Ring, ring.

"Hello?" The voice sounds like sandpaper: gritty. Like it hasn't been used in a while but knows it has a job to do now.

"Hi, this is Claire Barton." I clear my throat. "I'm in the seventh grade at Pebble Village School."

Across the loft, Maya gives me two thumbs-up. I turn toward the wall so I can't see her, even though having her nearby makes me feel better.

Then I completely forget everything I planned to say next. My silence grows like a welt.

But the sandpaper voice comes back. "Your teacher mentioned you'd be calling," it says. "I'm Mr. Hamilton. Ethan Hamilton."

I nod, even though he obviously can't see me. *Focus*, I tell myself. "Yes. Thank you. I, um—I wanted to ask you about Jack Hamilton. It's for a research project. About how people used to use horses."

Silence again. Then: "Your teacher might have told you that Jack Hamilton was my dad. How did you find out about him?"

I know I have to tell Mr. Hamilton about the box. It's not that I thought I could keep it a secret forever. But still, talking about it with someone I don't know feels strange, especially when I haven't even shown it to Andy yet.

"I found a box in my barn," I say.

"A box in your barn?" Mr. Hamilton's voice rises a little.

I nod again. Why do I keep nodding? It doesn't count for much over the phone. "Under a loose floorboard in the hayloft. I tripped over it." I read the article's headline and describe the picture.

Mr. Hamilton doesn't speak at first. Then he says: "That sounds interesting. Was there anything else in the box?"

I run my fingers over the curled leather, cracked and stiff. Over the cold bits and the heavy, smooth stone. One by one, I describe them all.

"Would you mind bringing the box with you when you visit?" Mr. Hamilton asks. "I'd be interested to see it."

I barely hear what he says next, about his address and when to arrive on Saturday morning. But I manage to thumb the details into a text message and send it to Mom and Dad.

When I press END, silence comes back into the barn. I lie against a hay bale, the box at my feet, and look up at the cobwebby ceiling, the braces joined together. A long time ago, before nails were easy to come by, somebody had made holes in all these pieces of wood and carved out pegs to fit perfectly in each one so they could stand together and prop up a whole barn.

"How'd it go?" Maya asks, settling into the hay next to me. "It sounded like you did awesome. Your voice didn't shake or anything."

"It felt different on the inside," I say.

"Nobody sees the inside." Maya's trying to help, like always, but her voice has that heavy sound again.

As I cradle the weight of the box, I think about how Maya's right. The outside never tells the whole story. Just looking at the box, nobody would ever know it meant anything at all.

I sit up and close the box gently until the metal cover clicks into place. "Hey. We should go on a ride."

"What?" Maya raises her eyebrows. "By ourselves?"

"Follow me." I climb down the ladder and stop by the door leading to Sunny's and Sam's stalls. "Mom and Dad let me ride by myself in the woods now."

Maya's jaw drops. "Are you kidding?"

"I convinced them," I say. "All I had to do was explain what Sharon said. She wanted us to figure out something we could do by ourselves, that we really liked."

"Well, yours would be pretty obvious," Maya says, gesturing around the barn. "You like being here."

"Yeah, but Mom's been coming to help with chores more lately, and I like to be by myself." I step into the stable. "So I told them I wanted to ride in the woods alone."

"Like, whenever you want?" Maya follows me into the stable.

"I mean, there are some rules." I take out my phone and start a text.

"Wait a second," Maya says. "If I went with you, you wouldn't technically be by yourself."

"Being with you counts," I say. Maya's voice has more lightness in it now, and I don't want to ruin that. "And riding always helps anyway."

"You're right," Maya says quietly. "It always does."

"Since I've been researching equine therapy so much, I've learned that people actually study this kind of stuff," I say. "Horses can help people with all kinds of issues: physical disabilities, developmental delays, emotional problems..."

"Emotional problems?" Maya asks. "How does that work?"

"Horses are kind of like mirrors that show what people are thinking and feeling," I explain.

Maya takes a deep breath. "Really?"

"They actually have a special membrane in their nose that allows them to sense human emotion," I explain. "You know how I've said before if I'm feeling upset about something, Sunny—but even Sam too—kind of acts weird? Like more jumpy?"

Maya nods. "They're like mind readers."

"Exactly. And it ends up being really helpful. Because horses can show people how their feelings are affecting their actions. And that helps people change certain patterns." I think of Sam's quiet eyes. "Maybe that's why I don't need to talk to feel better when I'm around horses."

I can't read Maya's face. She folds her arms across her chest.

"Hey," I say, nudging her with my elbow. "You good?"

Maya shrugs, and when she looks at me, her eyes crinkle with worry. "I don't even know, Claire," she says. "What you said about equine therapy and emotions—it made me think about Papi."

"Your dad likes horses?" I've never heard Mr. Gonzalez even ask about Sunny and Sam before.

"No, that's not it." Maya shakes her head. "He had to go to the doctor yesterday. Something to do with stress. He really isn't feeling well. My mom's worried."

"I'm sorry," I whisper.

To my surprise, Maya's eyes fill with tears. "I wish I knew how to help him."

"He'll be okay," I say.

Maya shakes her head. "How do you know that?"

I feel my cheeks redden. I hate saying the wrong thing. "Because he has to be."

Then, before Maya can ask anything else, I

stand up and hold out my hand. "Let's go," I say. Getting out in the woods will help us both feel better.

Maya wipes her eyes, then retrieves the brush box from the tack room and hands me a curry-comb. "So does this mean you'll be riding Sunny?"

I haven't ridden Sunny in a while. The last time was in the ring this summer, with Mom and Andy coaching me. Thinking about her springy ner-vousness as I tried to give her the right cues makes me wonder, for a second, if it's a good idea to try again.

But my urge to catch another glimpse of the wild horses, or to see if more stones like the silvery-black ones surrounding the cavern by the lake have found their way to the forest floor, crawls over my fear. "Totally," I say. "It's no problem."

"Okay," Maya says slowly, and we get the horses ready in silence.

I can feel Sunny's questions pulsing in every step we take outside. *Why are you here? Where are we going?* Her head moves jerkily up and down with each careful step. It feels like an electric current runs through her body. Under my legs she's tense, ready to burst at any moment.

"It's okay," I whisper, patting her neck, but my fingertips are as fluttery as sparrow wings. *Don't be nervous*, I tell myself. *If you're nervous, she'll be nervous.*

I know this, but it doesn't help much. I fill my stomach with air, then let it out again, trying to focus on the trees ahead instead of Sunny's trembling.

"Do you think we'll see them again?" Maya asks as we head into the woods.

"Definitely." I'm still not totally sure, but thinking about the possibility of the horses calms me, helps me refocus. I scan the woods, not just the whole of the forest but each tree, hoping for a swish of black circling the craggy bark of the white pine.

And then there it is: first the imprint of hooves in the leaves, then the unmistakable curve of silvery haunches weaving through trees. The rustle of tails in the wind.

They're here.

"Do you see them?" I ask Maya, pointing.

Her eyes widen. "Hang on," she says. "This time I think I sort of might."

We squint into the trees: The wild horses' noses touch, and they toss their heads.

Sunny and Sam stand perfectly still, but I don't feel the kind of tension that comes from rock-hard fear in their muscles. Their heads hang, calm and quiet.

I watch the wild horses, barely daring to breathe. They mince through the trees, their coats shining, the color of stars.

But then, in all that quiet, there's a clattering rush of sound: a pheasant. Pheasants always come out of nowhere. They nest on the ground and blend into the leaves and branches and dirt so well it's impossible to see them until they lurch into the air, clapping their wings.

I barely have time to register the pheasant before Sunny breaks into a run. This is no canter, no gentle rocking—I feel all four of her feet leaving the ground as she leaps forward. I hear Mom's and Andy's voices in my mind: *Turn her!* But no matter how I pull on the inside rein or how deep I sit, she won't slow. All I can do is hang on, never mind applying pressure from my right leg to try to bend her body around.

The world moves too fast for me to grab on to with my eyes or hands. Trees whip by in a blur of cherry, lemon, and orange. The path folds underneath pounding feet and the sky tilts crazily overhead, like it's about to spill all that blue on our heads. The dappled horses move with us at first, hooves rattling the ground, manes and tails streaming like flags in the cold air.

And then Sunny stops all of a sudden, at a point where the path in the woods splits. It's like she wore herself out and can't bring herself to go any farther, especially not into the darkness of thicker trees. The wild horses are gone, dissolved. Sunny breathes hard and I twist around, looking for any sign of what used to be there.

The moment my breath slows and I return to the feel of the saddle beneath me, Sunny's flanks still heaving, my heart seizes: *Maya*.

I hear her speak before my fear has a chance to grow.

"Claire!" Her voice has the trembly, frightened thrum of Sunny's legs, only those have finally quieted. Sunny's hanging her head so low her nose almost touches the matted leaves below. "Are you okay?"

I turn to see Maya sitting straight up on Sam's back, his walk slow and calm like always, as though nothing has happened, and I feel my shoulders slump in relief.

"I'm fine," I say, but my voice sounds so dry and quiet, almost a whisper. I clear my throat, then try again, louder: "Everything's fine."

"What happened?" Maya clenches Sam's reins, and her eyes flash, searching me over.

I shake my head. "Sunny got spooked." I press my heels into her side, just barely, enough to get her fully turned and walking next to Sam, toward home. "A pheasant."

"That freaked me out." Maya's voice shakes a little. "But Sam was really good. He just watched Sunny run. Finally, when you stopped, he started walking forward again. I lost track of the wild horses, though."

Relief melts through me, warm and sweet as Andy's mountain coffee. It was a close call. If Sam hadn't held it together, Maya could have gotten really hurt. I could have too. I was lucky.

"So you finally saw them!" Hopefully changing the subject will keep that relief flooding past the nervousness that still pricks cold and sharp.

"I think I might have," Maya says. "I saw something kind of silvery, but dark too."

"That's them." My heartbeat slows.

"I mean, I don't think I saw them as clearly as you did," Maya says, looking into the trees. "Where do you think they came from?"

I picture the boy's eyes from the old newspaper, dark and searching.

"I don't know," I say. "But I feel like they have something to do with Jack."

"Jack?" Maya's eyebrows wrinkle. "Wait—*that* Jack? The one from the article?"

"I know," I say. "I mean, I'm not saying they're *his*. They're not like hundred-year-old ghost horses. I just think the fact that I saw these wild horses, then found the box..." I trail off. How can

I explain the way the air shimmers when I touch the box or see the horses?

I started searching for the wild horses because of Andy, but finding them again and following where they lead feels as big somehow as one of the white pines towering far above me. It feels like I'm doing exactly what Sharon instructed: finding something that's all my own.

CHAPTER 12

"Almost ready?" Mom asks. She rubs her hands together and smiles. "You know, your dad was telling me he remembers Owen Hamilton from when he was younger. That would be Mr. Hamilton's son."

"I know, Mom." We already talked about this, but for some reason repeating it seems to make Mom feel better. It doesn't help me very much. I just end up thinking about how I'm going to have to talk to Mr. Hamilton in person now.

"Good guy," Dad says. "I used to hang out over at Owen's house in high school."

"And Mr. Hamilton never said anything to you about his father's accident with the horses?" I ask.

"Guess he wouldn't really have had a cause to," Dad says. "Most of the time, Owen and I were headed out to hunt or fish or go mudding. We were teenagers—we didn't sit around listening to his dad's old stories."

"You never saw any old pictures hanging up around the house either?" I ask. "Like of ancestors or something?" If Mr. Hamilton has any pictures of Jack, I'm sure I'll recognize him right away. Even in an old photo, his eyes shine bright as the silver-streaked stones.

"Not that I remember," Dad says.

Mom shakes her head. "I still can't believe that article."

When I showed it to her and Dad yesterday, I fibbed that I got it at the library because the box still feels too mysterious to share. They both squinted and scrunched their foreheads and tried to remember if they'd ever heard anything about Jack Hamilton, but his story didn't sound familiar to either of them.

"Good luck," Mom tells me. "And Claire—you'll do great."

I take the deep breath that's been helping more and more lately. And then I open the door.

The air outside stings a little. Every morning feels crisper now, colors still pretty but softer, fading, leaves falling like rain. I love how the air catches in my throat, how I have to breathe shallowly so its sharp edges don't cut too deep. People think of fall as a time when everything starts to die, but they just aren't paying attention. Coldness wakes me up.

Dad's already started the engine. Early frost coats the windshield and we lean over the hood from opposite sites, scraping crystals away. Working together, we get a clearer view.

In the car, Dad's quiet. He drives with one hand, his other hand squeezing the skin around his chin, his jaw working. We turn onto the dirt road that leads to Route 15, which curves around the mountains and past Pine Lake, then eventually veers off in two directions, the other leading to Cedar Lake and Belding:

I look up at the gray face of Pebble Mountain. A waterfall tumbles down, shining, clutching the rock with bony fingers.

"You have a good week, kiddo?" Dad fiddles with the radio dial, then turns it all the way off.

"I guess so." How can I sum up my week without talking about the box or the horses in the woods—or, more important, the pills and phone in Andy's closet? I'm not ready to tell Dad about any of those things. I only just mentioned the horses to Andy, and that didn't go the way I expected.

"What's on your mind?" Dad can always tell when I'm thinking hard.

"I guess I'm a little nervous about talking to Mr. Hamilton." Which is true—as curious as I am about Jack Hamilton and the box, having to sit next to a new person and talk for however long it will take me to get information doesn't sound fun. "I kind of miss Andy too," I add. Dad and I haven't talked about him in a while.

Dad's jaw clenches, a hard line. "He'll be back soon enough," he says. "In the meantime, he's got some learning to do."

His voice sounds harder than usual. Dad always said Andy was his right-hand guy and I was his right-hand girl. That he needed the both of us by his side. Sometimes it feels like he's changed his mind. But if he has, he wouldn't be the only one. Andy's changing too, and getting letters from him makes me feel more upside-down than excited these days.

Dad takes a ragged breath, and then I know maybe he's as confused as I am. "I miss him too, Claire," he says. "But I think he's right where he needs to be. For now."

We turn onto a narrow dirt drive choked with maples. Our truck bounces up and down in the ruts rain made, and Dad takes it slow. The drive-way feels long, but it empties into a clearing with a small ranch house ahead and a large barn on the right. A cedar-pole fence, crooked in spots but strong, rings a pasture twice the size of ours, but I don't see any horses. No hay tossed on the frozen ground. No water trough. Even from the outside, the barn feels empty.

Dad pulls the truck up and turns off the engine. "Well," he says. "Ready?"

I nod and pull my backpack over my shoulders, the box weighing it down.

Dad walks to the house first.

"Wait!" I can feel the sparrows flying in already, pulsing their wings. "Wait a second."

But Dad lifts his finger and presses the bell. "It's best to get started, Claire, honey," he says, holding his hand up for a high five. "You'll be fine."

The sparrows rustle wildly then, and their little feet skitter under my skin. I push my palm against Dad's and he squeezes, filling me with some warmth just as the door opens and a man with wispy gray hair and skin the color of straw fills the frame. A shaggy dog threads itself between his legs and rushes out.

"Taffy!" the man says sharply. "Taffy, stop that, now."

But as soon as I see his dog, the sparrows begin to settle. I stand perfectly still on the doorstep, keeping my eyes low and my palms open for her to smell.

I feel Taffy's heart quieting as she loops around

me, her nose pushing my ankles. I stroke her head and rub her furry chin.

"Welcome, Claire," Mr. Hamilton says. "That dog's not too fond of strangers, but it looks like she approves of you."

"I love animals," I say, standing up to shake Mr. Hamilton's hand. I look quickly at his eyes, because I know I'm supposed to. But I feel better looking at Taffy.

"Well, come on in," Mr. Hamilton says, then looks at Dad. "It's good to see you again, George. Been a long time. You're all grown up."

Dad laughs, then takes Mr. Hamilton's hand. "Yes. How's Owen?"

"Busy in Boulder," Mr. Hamilton says. "Different world out there."

"Sure must be." Dad steps in, but lingers in the doorway. "We'll have to catch up, but I want to be sure Claire gets her interview done first."

"How about we talk out on the side porch?" Mr. Hamilton says. "I still have screens in the windows to catch the fresh air. It's a little chilly, but the sun's shining now, and we might not have too many more days like this."

"Perfect," Dad says. "I'll take a stroll around those nice fields you have past the porch. I know Claire would prefer doing the interview without me hovering just over her shoulder."

"It can be hard to talk to a new person," Mr. Hamilton says, so quietly the sparrows calm even more, their wings making only the tiniest flutters. I can tell they'll fly away soon. "Feel free to join us anytime, or explore."

"I might take a look around your barn too," Dad says.

"Have at it." Mr. Hamilton leads us through his living room and out to the screened-in porch, where autumn sun bathes the walls in gold. "Not much there anymore. Not like you remember."

"Things change." Dad taps me on the shoulder. "I'll check back in soon, Claire. Ten minutes?"

"Fifteen should be good." I want enough time to show Mr. Hamilton the box without Dad walking in and seeing it. It's not that I want to keep it a secret forever. I just need to figure out exactly when and what to tell him. Dad nods, then steps out the porch door and strolls toward the fields.

Mr. Hamilton gestures for me to follow him to one end of the porch, which is crammed with plants and overstuffed furniture. A cat walks delicately across the top of the couch, its tail high in the air.

"Move over, Mitzi." Mr. Hamilton lifts the cat gently, extracting her claws from the fabric, and sets her on the floor. She stalks to my feet and starts to purr.

I perch on the edge of a chair opposite the couch and stroke Mitzi's head.

"So," Mr. Hamilton says, "you have some questions for me."

"A few," I say. "Do you mind if I record you?"

"Nothing to hide here," Mr. Hamilton says. "I guess I have a question for you first, though. I know you told me what was in that box, but could I take a look at it, please? If you brought it, that is."

I open my backpack, pulling the box out. "I haven't shown it to my parents yet."

"I'm sure they've never seen it before," Mr.

Hamilton says. "It was your mom's great-grandfather who bought that farm from my grandparents. She wouldn't have known their last names from that long ago."

"Wait," I say. Wind swoops through my chest, scattering the sparrows. "Our house used to belong to the Hamiltons? Jack used to *live* there?"

I had barely dared to think it. But it turns out I was right.

Mr. Hamilton nods. "No reason for your mom to know that kind of connection, though. It was a long time ago." He reaches for the box and runs his hand over the top, then blinks a few times, staring like it's a block of gold. Slowly, he lifts the lid.

"Wow," he says, so softly it sounds like a breath instead of a word.

"You've seen it before?" Suddenly I remember when I was in second grade and lost my favorite doll for a whole winter. I only found her in spring when the snow finally finished melting and I saw I'd dropped her in the garden, in between rows of thick kale we'd left in the ground after it got cold.

Mr. Hamilton's looking at the box just like I looked at my doll.

But he shakes his head. "Only heard about it," he says. "My dad—that's Jack, from the picture you found—would talk about it sometimes, especially as he got old, but honestly, I just thought he was confused. Pretty much everyone did, toward the end."

"Why did they think that?" I can't imagine hearing about the box and not wanting to at least look for it.

"After Dad's accident, the whole family was completely rattled," Mr. Hamilton says. "Dad maybe most of all. Didn't want any part of that old place anymore. Thought it was bad luck."

"Where did they go?" I ask.

"They bought this place instead." Mr. Hamilton gestures out the window at the barn, the fences, the evergreens beyond. "Worked any way they could without horses. Had some milk cows once, raised some pigs. My grandfather—that would be Jack's dad—worked in the mill for a while."

"So if they left," I say, "how did this box get into our barn?"

Mr. Hamilton smiles. "For that, I need to rewind a little ways," he says, and holds up the article. "This tells you Jack's horses fell through the ice—so they died, right?"

"Of course." It makes me sad to think about the horses slipping away, but at least Jack was lucky to live.

Mr. Hamilton's sandpaper voice gets so soft I have to strain to hear him. "Well, my dad thought they didn't." He chuckles to himself, shakes his head. "I never believed it—still don't. But Dad—Jack—he was convinced they figured out a way to escape."

I feel something surge through me, and it isn't the sparrows with their nervous flutter and frantic song. It's something stronger. It's a wave, a glittering push and pull, and I lean forward, ready to listen.

CHAPTER 13

"Horses couldn't survive that icy water." I shake my head, trying to figure out how the pieces fit.

"I agree," Mr. Hamilton says, holding his hands up. "Like I said, Dad's stories never made sense to me, but I do remember one he always shared about the summer three months after his accident. He had a boat out on Pine Lake and was trying to catch some perch, when he saw something in the water."

Mr. Hamilton shakes his head, looks down again at the bits, then lifts the leather harness piece out of the box. "He told me he paddled closer and saw...well, exactly what we're looking at right here. Bits and harness. Just floating."

My brain scrambles to calculate. Bits are solid metal, and leather absorbs every inch of water—that's why harnesses and tack get heavier when they're wet. They'd never float.

"Ever since the accident," Mr. Hamilton continues, "all my dad wanted was evidence that the horses hadn't died. He was just a kid when it happened. Believing the horses were really gone was probably too painful."

"So...what did he do?" I ask.

"Well, he reeled in his line and forgot about fishing, at least for the time being," Mr. Hamilton says. "Then he headed over to where he saw the bits and harness floating, and he picked them up."

Mr. Hamilton grabs the harness piece and unrolls it. He freezes for a second, and his eyes get wide. But then he chuckles. "Leave it to Dad to come up with the most harebrained possible explanation." He glances back at me. "I don't know how carefully you looked at this when you found it in the box. Did you see what's etched in the corner?"

He holds the leather out toward me, and I hesitate just a moment before taking it. I squint at the spot where Mr. Hamilton's finger points and see a letter: *H*. Someone had carved it, maybe with a knife point. The edges aren't perfect, but it's there for sure.

"Dad always told me he knew the leather had come from his harness before he even pulled it out of the water," Mr. Hamilton says. "But he turned it over to make sure, and when he saw that *H*, he knew it was his. So he brought that and the bits into the boat and sat there for a while, wondering what to do next."

"Wait." I'd been thinking so hard about how tack could be floating in the first place when Mr. Hamilton told that part of the story that it still hadn't really sunk in. Now it does. "You're saying Jack found the leather and bits in Pine Lake, right? That's near my house. But didn't the horses fall through the ice on *Cedar* Lake? That's all the way over in Belding."

Mr. Hamilton smiles. "First of all," he says, "you should know that Dad's imagination stretched, well"—he raises one hand above his head and taps the air—"pretty much this high. But yes, according to him, these items in the box proved the horses escaped Cedar Lake and ended up miles away, exactly like you said."

"How?" Images of the lakes shimmer. I've been swimming in them as long as I can remember. Every birthday party I had was a barbecue on one of the beaches, the smell of charcoal heating in the little grills set up under the trees, sand sticking to our wet feet and fingers. We'd look out at the water and it seemed so easy to know what it was, top to bottom. What if I was missing something the whole time?

But Mr. Hamilton's already shaking his head. "Who knows? He never could quite explain that part. I remember him saying the horses must have scrambled out somehow and made it to shore, then pushed over the mountain to Pine Lake and walked across—it would've still been frozen—to get into the woods."

"It doesn't seem possible," I say, but everything

inside me says it *must* be. I remember the part of Pine Lake I hadn't expected to find. Clusters of stones ringing a circle of darkness, where waves push against sand. What's beyond that darkness? Where does it lead?

Mr. Hamilton laughs. "I definitely wouldn't call it possible. I'd call it a good story, told by a person who needed one. Any psychologist today would probably say it was a response that helped my dad cope with the trauma of his accident."

"But what if he was right?" I ask. "Nobody ever proved the horses died for certain, right? Nobody ever found them?"

Mr. Hamilton's eyes sparkle. "I'm not sure how hard they looked, but Dad did like to say there were always hidden paths. Ways out and through nearly anything, even when people didn't want to see them. Sounds like you two might look at the world in about the same way."

I do like the idea of a way out. A path I could find, made just for me.

"Let's say it's true." My voice sounds louder, stronger. "Why wouldn't the harness be attached to the horses anymore? How would they have gotten them off?"

"Dad figured they helped each other out somehow," Mr. Hamilton says. "Probably bit the leather clean through as they were crossing the ice. If they did, snow would've covered what they left behind pretty quick, so at least the part about not finding anything until summer, when the snow was long gone, makes sense."

"Wouldn't the horses have come back to Jack eventually, though?" I can't imagine Sunny and Sam getting lost and not finding their way home, no matter how long it took.

"I asked him that," Mr. Hamilton says. "But Dad used to shrug and tell me they must have found freedom in the woods, and liked it. He never seemed to begrudge them that."

I imagine the horses running away, their wet tails streaming.

But I don't think they pulled themselves back onto what was left of Crystal Lake's ice. I don't think that's how they got away.

It's hard to believe that two horses could make

their way from one lake to the other unnoticed, even as inky dark crept over the winter evening. Even if they *had* somehow stumbled up the stony bank and wandered over frozen corn stubble, then over the forested Pebble Mountain...there would have been some evidence left behind. Hoofprints, maybe. Someone would have seen.

They must have escaped another way.

"What about the stone?" I pick it up, roll it in my palm.

Mr. Hamilton looks surprised.

"Even if Jack's story isn't true," I continue, "I get why he kept the bits and harness piece. They're something to remember the horses by. But what does a stone have to do with it?"

"You're asking good questions," Mr. Hamilton says. "Exactly what an interviewer should do. I'm sorry I don't have better answers, because I don't remember Dad telling me about the stone. It's certainly a beautiful one." Then he shrugs. "Dad was a bit of a collector. Could have been something he found that he just wanted to keep, though it doesn't look like the rocks I've seen around here."

My legs tingle. All I want is to return to the woods and find that ring of stones again. I think the darkness carved out of that hill by the beach could explain how Jack's horses escaped. And how wild horses, so many years later, still live half hidden in the trees.

"Do you think that maybe his story could be true?" I ask. "Now that you've seen the box, I mean?"

Mr. Hamilton smiles and bounces the stone lightly in his palms. He opens his mouth to speak, then closes it again and shakes his head. Mitzi leaps up onto his lap, and he strokes her back while she purrs.

"It's funny," he says. "This is the box Dad always told me about. He said he hid it up there, in the barn that used to belong to his family, so the story checks out in that regard. But finding it just means that yes, he tucked something away for safekeeping before his family moved. It doesn't prove all the rest."

"But these have to be his." I point at the worn *H* in the leather. "That's not just anybody's."

"Sure." Mr. Hamilton nods and holds the strap up, letting it dangle from his fingers. "But remember, the family stopped using horses after the accident. It's not like they were taking great care of their tack anymore. Dad could've found this stuff anywhere, before they left the farm. He could have made it fit any story he wanted."

"Do you think he hid something in your barn too?" I ask, glancing out the window. I see Dad still walking the fence line, his hands stuffed in his pockets. "Because this is where he moved to, right? This is where you grew up?"

"Yes," Mr. Hamilton says. "But like I told you, the family stopped working with horses, and I know that was hard for my dad. Might be why he spun so many stories about them. Couldn't get them out of his head. There wouldn't have been much around for him to hide."

I hear my voice swimming through thickened air, and I realize I haven't felt the wisp of feathers since we started talking. "Do you want me to look anyway?"

CHAPTER 14

Sun glistens, turning leaves into gems: ruby, emerald, topaz. I try to keep up with Mr. Hamilton. He might be old, but he moves fast.

Dad waves at us from the entrance to the barn, and I jog over to meet him.

"How'd the interview go, kiddo?" He pulls me into a quick hug.

"It was really...interesting," I say. Thoughts gather, rustling thick like leaves.

Dad claps Mr. Hamilton on the back. "Thanks for taking your time. Every once in a while I looked back and saw you two chatting through the screen. Looked like you had lots to discuss."

"Claire is a great conversationalist," Mr. Hamilton says. "She kept me on my toes."

Dad smiles, but I can tell he's holding in a laugh. I don't blame him. I'm not sure anybody but Maya and Andy would call me a "conversationalist." But with Mr. Hamilton, talking wasn't so bad. Somehow all my wanting to know about Jack and the horses rested on the sparrows like a gentle hand and kept them quiet.

I twist the door latch open. The warm dark of this barn feels exactly like mine, and it smells the same too: like dry hay and sweet grain and sawdust gathered in piles.

"She's not shy about some things," I hear Dad telling Mr. Hamilton as I step inside and get my bearings. Instinctively I reach for a light switch on the wall, and a sticky yellow glow fills the barn.

On my right are two rows of stalls, dusty and gray, a concrete aisle running between. I glimpse what could definitely be a tack room at the end of the row of stalls, and is that a saddle horn, just

visible inside the half-open door? There's no milk-
ing parlor like I'd expect for cows, or chicken wire
or cages for rabbits or anything else. This looks
like a barn for horses.

It takes me a while to register what I see on the
left, but as soon as I do, I have to catch my breath.
It's small for what it is, but there's no mistaking:
It's a completely closed-in, weatherproof riding
arena. A fence circles soft dirt, and I even think
I can see the leftover prints of hooves, deep and
shadowed.

Dad's voice floats in behind me. "Can you
imagine having one of these in the winter?" he asks.

A hot, sharp feeling works its way into my
chest, like I wish Mr. Hamilton could lift his barn
up and bring it to me or someone else who could
fill it with the animals it was meant for.

All I can do is nod, and Dad squeezes my shoulder. "Maybe one day," he says, but I hear how he
swallows the last word down hard, and he looks
quickly away. I guess he almost forgot what I wish
weren't true: that we're not going to be needing an
indoor riding arena. Without Sunny and Sam, we

won't even need the little outdoor one we have. It will sit empty, and if the roof doesn't get repaired it will clog with snow in winter, and in summer the switchgrass will start to crowd the dirt Dad laid down and it won't look like anything at all.

Mr. Hamilton comes up beside me and leans his forearms against the fence bordering the arena.

"I thought Jack didn't have horses," I say. "I mean, I thought *you* didn't have horses either. You said his parents—"

"They didn't," Mr. Hamilton says. "But I did."

"What?!" My jaw drops.

"I thought I told you that, Claire," Dad says.

"Um, no!" I blurt, louder than I mean to. I spin on my heel and point to Dad. "You just told me about how you and Owen liked to go fishing instead of listening to Mr. Hamilton's stories. Which are really interesting, by the way!"

Mr. Hamilton bursts out laughing. "Well, thanks. But I don't blame the boys for preferring fishing."

"I do remember watching you in here a few times, working one of the three-year-olds people would bring you to train," Dad says to Mr. Hamilton. "You knew what you were doing."

"I suppose I must have." Mr. Hamilton's eyes twinkle.

Where are they now? I wonder. How could a horse trainer like Mr. Hamilton not have horses?

Mr. Hamilton must see the question slide across my face, because he catches my eyes with his and smiles. "My grandkids love horses," he says. "But when Owen got that new job out West, and they couldn't come around anymore, eventually I stopped seeing the point in keeping mine. I was getting tired too. I'm old, you know."

"Don't you miss the horses?" I ask.

"Hmmm." Mr. Hamilton looks up at the ceiling for a second. Scratches his chin. "To be perfectly honest, I try not to think about it that much."

"Horses are a lot of work," Dad says.

"They are." Mr. Hamilton nods. "But I'll admit, not having them anymore has been—an adjustment."

Wings flutter at my shoulder. *Not now,* I think. When Mr. Hamilton said "not having them anymore," all I could think of was Sunny and Sam. "I'm going to look around," I say.

I take my time, breathing deeply to push the wings away. I open creaky stall doors, brush spiderwebs from feed buckets, run my hands over saddles and bridles so dusty my fingers turn gray.

But there isn't much here. Not anymore. And there's definitely nothing else even close to the box. If Jack Hamilton hid anything else, I don't think it was here.

Still, I can't help peering into a few corners. I'm tipping up the feed bin, counting specks of old grain left at the bottom, when Dad says it's time to go.

"Thanks, Mr. Hamilton." I shake his hand, my grip strong, the sparrows finally gone.

"Thank *you*, Claire," he says. "I hope I helped you with your project, but I would be glad to talk again if you'd like."

The word *project* brings heat rushing to my face. I realize that even though I learned a lot about the box, and what it might mean, I didn't really talk to Mr. Hamilton about my research topic. "That would be great."

But as we walk to the car, I don't think about my project. Instead, I wonder about Jack. *Was he right? Did the horses survive? And if so, how?* The questions spin in my head, pressing against my eyelids as I shut them tight and lean against the headrest in Dad's truck.

"Buckled?" Dad asks, turning the key in the ignition. I click my seat belt and turn to look out the rear window as we drive away. Mr. Hamilton's still standing where we said goodbye at the barn door. I watch him raise one steady hand before striding toward the house, and I wave back as we turn down the driveway.

There aren't many cars on our roads, which curve like pencil lines around the mountains and the water. It's possible, if you time it right, to drive all the way from Cedar Lake to my house in perfect quiet, without seeing anyone else.

Dad clears his throat. "What did you think of Mr. Hamilton?"

I turn from the window and watch the steering wheel slide through his hands. "I like him. I can't believe you didn't tell me he used to have horses."

"Yeah. I thought I did." He rubs his chin, then looks quickly at me before turning back to the road. His voice gets quiet. "Actually, you know what, I probably avoided telling you without even realizing it. I didn't want it to get you thinking about Sunny and Sam."

My eyes pinch and burn. "I was going to learn about his horses sooner or later."

Dad sighs. "I know. I guess I wanted to put it off."

My throat tightens, but I squeeze the words out anyway. "It's just not fair, Dad."

We both know I'm not talking about Mr. Hamilton's horses anymore.

"I'm sorry, Claire." Dad's voice sounds thick, tired. "I really am. Your mom and I can't see a way to make it work."

A tear rolls down my cheek and I wipe it away.

"Hey," Dad says. "We'll get through it. Hard things like this—there's always another side." Suddenly he presses the brake and pulls the car over at a turnoff. Then he points out the window. "What's that?"

From here, it just looks like a wall of stone. But I know what it really is. "Pebble Mountain. Obviously."

"We're so close to it here, though, you can't see the top even if you look up," Dad says. "Right?"

I nod, the muscly granite blurring beyond the glass.

"But you've hiked all the way up before," he continues. "So you know it's there. Our house is on the other side, so you know that's there too. Right?"

I nod, wipe my eyes again.

"Sometimes when you're right up close to something, you can't see the whole of it. But there's always more," Dad says, taking my hand. "I promise."

He presses on the gas and we move forward, around the road as it bends. I don't want to let go of Dad's hand, and he lets me hold it while he drives.

Then my phone buzzes with a text from Maya.

I let go of Dad's hand and write back.

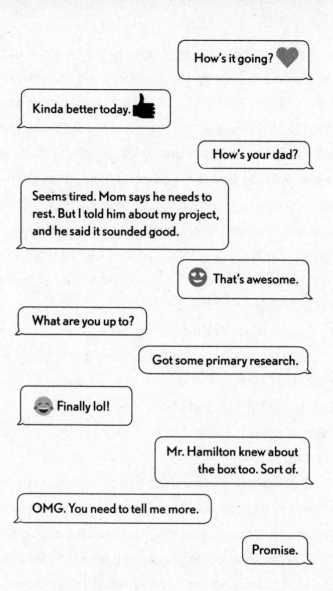

How's it going? 🖤

Kinda better today. 👍

How's your dad?

Seems tired. Mom says he needs to rest. But I told him about my project, and he said it sounded good.

😄 That's awesome.

What are you up to?

Got some primary research.

😂 Finally lol!

Mr. Hamilton knew about the box too. Sort of.

OMG. You need to tell me more.

Promise.

I slide the phone back in my pocket.

Outside the window, pieces of my world flash by: the Moores' dairy farm, with its big white barn and silo; the Jordans' little ranch house with the yard full of ceramic ornaments and bikes and the kennel out back where they keep sled dogs; the now stubbly fields where in summer corn grows; the surface of Pine Lake, rippling blue and gray. That means we're getting closer to my house, and also to the spot at the intersection of Route 15 and Mountain Trail Road where Andy used to drive us to hike up Pebble Mountain.

The flutter feeling comes back when I think about Andy. How much more time until he'll be back safe at home, sitting in the kitchen, scrolling through his phone and looking up, saying, "Hey, Little C.," trying to pretend he hasn't left me behind?

But Andy doesn't want to come home. And even if he did, what would he find here? Would he come looking for the bag of pills in the closet? Would he charge the strange phone and keep it hidden in his coat pocket where nobody could see it? A tiny spark of the hot feeling I had when I thought about

Mr. Hamilton's barn sitting empty flickers inside. If I kindled it, I know it would grow.

The sparrows swirl and tumble and bump into one another as they fly. I clasp my hands together and breathe, trying to steady their beating wings.

CHAPTER 15

"Letting go," Sharon says. "That's the idea I want all of you to think about as you leave today. What does it look like? How can it help you? This week, look for little ways to let go."

Sharon's closing words feel like a blanket that settles over all of our shoulders. None of us move at first. Then, slowly, kids get up and start milling around, grabbing cookies and juice from the table.

"You're Claire, right?" Anna asks, tucking a strand of hair behind her ear.

Little flutters hover at the base of my skull, but

I concentrate on answering Anna. "Yeah." I feel my cheeks redden. "I know I never say anything. Doesn't make it easy to remember who I am."

"No worries," Marcus says. "It took me ages to talk."

"Really?" I ask. Last week Marcus spoke so easily, shared so much, it's hard to imagine him struggling.

"You thought none of us would be able to relate, right?" Caleb says. He's smiling, but not in a mean way.

"Basically." Marcus smiles. "Seems funny now."

I look down at my shoes. It feels like if I meet any of their eyes, they'll all know that's exactly how *I've* felt. That's why I haven't talked.

"Man, we all thought that when we first started coming," Caleb says. "Then we kinda realized we're all in the same boat after all."

"So, Claire," Anna says. "Is it okay if I ask who in your family has the addiction issue?"

Sparrows flicker around my heart. "My brother."

The other kids nod. It makes me feel like I can say a little more. "He takes pain pills," I explain.

"I mean, he's addicted to them. Or was addicted. I don't know. I mean, he got hurt in this accident, with his snowmobile."

"Those pills are really strong," Caleb says.

"I found so many bottles of them in his closet," I say. "It's like he was saving them."

The other kids look at one another, almost as though they're nervous. I can't quite read their eyes.

"Maybe that's it," Marcus says quietly.

"It's definitely cool that you're here, Claire," Anna says. "You should keep coming."

"Thanks." Anna's words, Caleb's, Marcus's, they all feel good. Like Sharon's. Being in the same boat with them doesn't seem like the worst thing.

As we're heading up the steps to leave, Nari taps my shoulder. "Hey, Claire," she says. "I remembered what you said about your horses. Sunny and Sam, right?"

I stop walking, turn to face her. "You have a good memory!"

"They've been in my head off and on, ever since last week. I haven't really wanted to think much about my sister, but talking to you made me wonder why she started liking horses so much." She takes a deep breath. "And, okay, Sharon's basically forcing us to figure out all these ways to let go, right? Well, I figure this might be mine."

"What do you mean?" I ask.

"Fear," Nari says. "I told you I was scared of horses, right?"

I nod.

"Well," she says, taking a deep breath. "I think it's time to let go."

"How about tomorrow after school?" I ask.

Nari sticks out her hand. "It's a date."

When I get home the next day, Nari and her mom are already there, sitting at the table with Mom. Nari said her mom would drive her over; they must not have had any trouble with the directions I gave.

Mom's leaning forward, talking in a low voice, but when she sees me she stops in the middle of her sentence and smiles. "I'm so glad you invited these ladies over, Claire!"

Nari's mom has long hair the silvery-dark color of the stones. "It's so nice to meet you, Claire," she says. "I'm Ms. Datta. Nari is very excited to see your horses."

"I'm glad she could come," I say, shaking her hand. It's warm and soft, and she squeezes tight.

"Horses have been so helpful for our daughter Pia," Ms. Datta says. "We're actually not quite sure what we're going to do when she comes home and doesn't have them around anymore."

I want to tell her she can bring Pia to see our horses, but I haven't even told Andy or my parents about my equine therapy plan yet. My own thoughts about Andy feel like the sparrows now: tumbling, flighty, ready to burst.

"Do you want to see them too?" I ask.

"That would be fun." Ms. Datta wraps both her hands around her coffee mug and looks at Mom. "But I'm going to talk with your mother for a bit."

"I forced her into a conversation," Mom says, and she smiles again: a deep, real smile. I can tell she really likes Ms. Datta.

Ms. Datta laughs. "It's a pleasure, honestly."

"Nari, we should get going," I say. "This is when I usually do all my chores."

"I'll follow you," Nari says, and we head out the door.

The sun feels so warm, I peel my gloves off and stick them in my pocket.

"So you do this every day?" she asks. "Take care of the horses, I mean?"

"Yeah," I say. "I mean, my mom helps sometimes. But I really like to do it myself."

"Will I be in your way?" Nari waits behind as I push the barn door open.

"Oh no, I didn't mean it like that." I motion for her to follow me inside. "It's fun to have a friend here. It's just that my mom always wants to...I don't know. Talk about everything."

Nari laughs. "Oh yeah, there's always something to 'process,' right? Like about your brother?"

It feels kind of strange to laugh about Andy, but it also feels good to be with someone who knows exactly what I'm going through.

"Especially lately," I say, then almost wish

I hadn't. Nari doesn't seem to react. I lead her toward the stable, but she stops in the doorway.

"Whew," she says. "I don't know why I'm so nervous. Actually, I do. Like I told you, horses have always scared me."

"No problem," I say. Interestingly, the fact that Nari's nervous doesn't bring my sparrows back. Instead, I feel totally calm. "We'll start slow."

I bring Nari to Sam's stall and let her look at him from a couple of feet away.

"He's really huge," Nari says, her eyes wide.

"Horses are big," I say. "But a well-trained horse like Sam is also very gentle. One good thing to know about horses is they are prey animals, and their natural instinct is to run away when threatened."

"So they get nervous too." Nari laughs shakily.

"Exactly," I say. "But if we're relaxed, it helps them feel relaxed because they know they're safe."

Nari takes a deep breath. "Okay."

"I'm going to bring Sam out," I say. "You can wait over here at the wall, then I'll bring you over to meet him."

I look up at Sam and scratch between his ears

as I clip his cross-ties. "I'm going to have you approach him at an angle, from the front," I tell Nari. "Remember, Sam is really gentle. When you get near his head, put out your hand for him to catch your scent."

"Will he bite?" Nari asks, her voice rising.

"No way," I assure her. "Here, I'll put my hand out with yours."

Sam snuffles around Nari's palm, taps it lightly with his lips.

"He likes you," I say. Nari smiles.

Next, I hand her a currycomb and demonstrate how to move it in circles over Sam's shoulders, flanks, and back.

"Does your brother like horses too?" she asks.

Thinking about Andy and horses makes me feel like there's a heavy stone in my stomach. "He always did," I say quietly. "Lately he seems totally different. His letters are…weird. I don't really know how to get him back to being himself."

Nari stops brushing and looks at me. "I don't think my sister will ever be herself again. Hey, by the way, he's really soft." She pats Sam on the neck.

"Doesn't that bother you?" I ask. "Thinking that she'll totally change?"

"No." Nari's eyes glimmer with pain. She shakes her head like she's trying to make her answer true. "I don't let it. But my parents don't like that. They want me to support her. They say it's part of being a family. I just feel like it won't work."

"Yeah, I have no idea what will work with my brother either." I hand Nari a hard brush and show her how to swipe dusty loose hairs away from Sam's back and flanks.

"One thing my mom always says is that we all have to walk this path together," Nari says, pressing down on the brush. "It may or may not look the way we expected it to."

"I like that," I say. "And it makes sense. Wouldn't you miss your sister if she never came back?"

Nari chews her lip, looks away. "When you put it that way," she says softly, "yes. Of course I would. But I'm also frustrated with her."

"It makes sense that you would be." I picture the pills, the phone. But I don't feel like talking more about either of them right now, so I clip a lead rope to Sam's halter. "Do you want to learn how to lead a horse? You can help me bring him to the arena for lunging."

"Lunging?" Nari's eyes narrow in confusion.

"It's a way to exercise horses," I explain. "But also a good way to train."

I show Nari how to stand on Sam's left side, holding the lead rope in two places. Together, we slowly move out of the stable. Walking toward the arena, I gradually distance myself from Nari until she's leading Sam all by herself.

"This is a lot easier than I thought it would be," she says. "I actually kind of like it. I can't believe he's following me."

"When you want him to stop so you can hand the lead rope off to me, stand still and pull a little if he keeps moving," I say. "But the halter actually puts pressure on his nose and keeps him following your lead."

As soon as Nari stops, Sam does too. She turns to him, pets his nose, and smiles. When I come up to take the lead rope, she waits an extra second before letting go.

"Wasn't that bad, huh?" I ask.

Nari shakes her head. "Sam's really nice."

In our arena, Nari stands next to me, watching as I bring Sam to a trot. I listen to his hooves beat on dirt and wish everything could be that steady.

"So does your sister want to come back home?" I ask. "Or is she having too much fun with the horses?"

"I'm not sure," Nari says quietly, "but you know, this isn't the first time Pia's had to go to rehab."

"What?" I look quickly at her, then turn my eyes back to Sam.

"She was at a different place last year," Nari says. "She seemed okay at first. But then things got hard again."

The flutter feeling stirs in the pit of my stomach. "What do you mean?" I ask. "The rehab didn't help at all?"

"I'm not saying that," Nari explains. "It helped in some ways. My parents really like this new place, though. Pia told them that working with the horses makes her feel better than she has in a long time. Addiction is just hard. I mean, it's a disease, and there isn't one clear way to fix it. So it's not something you can be totally done with."

"I thought the whole point of rehab was to fix the problem," I say. Sam slows down, and I make a kissing sound to get him going.

"When you use the word *fix*, you make it sound like Pia's a broken motor or something," Nari says. "People aren't that simple, you know?"

"Sorry. I didn't mean—" I shake my head, blush. "So, she'll need to work on staying healthy, like, forever?" I make Sam change directions and watch his strong legs move.

"I guess," Nari says. "But you say that like it's a bad thing. Everybody has to work on stuff. Don't you?"

I think of the sparrows, swooping into every corner of me. The deep breaths I've learned to take to send them away, until the next time they appear.

Suddenly I feel tired enough to lie down in the leaves. All along, I've hoped that things with Andy could go back to being exactly like they used to be, but I don't know what that truly was anymore. Did I really know my brother? Do I now? I let Sam slow to a walk and bring him into the center of the circle he made. I stroke his nose.

"There are lots of people who figure out how to deal with addiction," Nari says. "Like Sharon, remember?"

"Sharon?" My jaw drops.

"You must not have been there when she told us," Nari says. "Maybe that was before you came. She's been sober for twenty years or something."

"But...isn't our group for people who have family members with that...problem?" I picture Sharon's calm eyes and jangling silver bracelets.

"I mean, yeah, but Sharon's mom had the same issue," Nari says. "So she needed to figure out how to deal with that. From both sides, see? It doesn't have to be one or the other."

Clouds sweep across the mountains. The gray feels calm and a little sad as it settles down. It matches my mind, swirling thick with questions I can't find words for.

I show Nari how to hold the lunge line tight enough so Sam will feel direction from my hand, but loose enough so he can trot in a wide circle.

"Here, try," I tell her.

Nari shakes her head. "I don't know," she says. "Leading him was probably enough."

"I'll stand behind you and help," I say, positioning myself so I can hold the lunge line. "He'll probably do what you want. But if he doesn't, that's when we tighten the pressure. You'll bump his nose a little with your hand, get him to listen."

Nari nods, her eyes focused on Sam.

Andy's the one who taught me that, leaning over my shoulder while I hung on to the line and tried to will Sam into doing what I wanted. Andy said it wasn't only horses who want to move away from pressure. *People are the same way, Little C. Think about it.*

"As soon as Sam does what we want, we'll let him go," I say. Nari turns toward me, confused. "Oh, I don't mean drop the rope, I just mean—give him more slack."

"Okay, yeah. I get it now," she says.

Pressure. Who wants that? Pressure comes when I have to talk to someone loud or new, stand up in a room full of staring people, face a thing that's not turning out like I thought it would. It stirs the sparrows from somewhere outside me, brings them inside, makes my fingers quiver so I have to squeeze my hands into fists to still them.

But it also makes me move forward.

"I think he's good," Nari says, and I realize I haven't even been watching Sam. I'm looking at the mountains beyond the arena instead, how they rise and rise, pushing past everything else to get where they're going. Sam's holding his pace, and I give Nari a thumbs-up.

"So what do you think?" I ask. "Can you see why your sister likes working with horses so much?"

"Actually, yeah," Nari says. "I'm holding this lunge line and it's literally the only thing I'm thinking about. Kind of helps me focus. I don't have much time to feel scared of the horses. Or of other things, actually."

I tell Nari about my equine therapy plan, and her eyes widen. "Seriously?" she asks. "Pia would be your first customer."

"Well, we have to see," I say. "I haven't told my

brother about it yet. And it all depends what he and my parents decide. I can't do it myself."

Thinking about what Andy might say fills me with wings and fire and all kinds of feelings I can't name. Nari's telling me that what happened with Andy will always be with us, in a way. But also that it's supposed to be okay. *Can* be okay.

"Hmmm," Nari says. "You might want to think about a plan B, in case he doesn't want to be part of it. Personally, I have no idea what to expect from my sister."

I picture the paths weaving through our forest, the one leading to Pine Lake. So many to choose— too many, maybe.

I don't want to think about Andy's path if it's not right next to mine.

In my room at night, I line up the materials I need. Paper, envelope, stamp. Everything's ready to go. Sitting down and touching the smooth stationery feels like running a brush down Sam's back: easy and steady, something I could do in my sleep.

I might have only one more chance. Andy might not believe me about the wild horses, but if I explain it well enough, he'll see that equine therapy is perfect for our family. He has to. If he'd been there with Nari, if he'd seen how much better she felt about horses when she left, he'd understand. I pick up my favorite pen, the one that drips smooth blue ink at just the right speed for letter writing.

I write on the envelope first: I know the address by heart. Then I set the blank paper in front of me. The words come easily.

> Dear Andy,
>
> Guess what? I have an idea.
>
> You know those meetings Mom and Dad make me go to? At the last one I heard about something kind of cool.

I have to think about how to phrase this next part. I'm sure Andy will like my idea—how could he not? But I don't want him to think I'm trying to *force* him to help. He'd probably tear my letter into little pieces. And besides, that's not it at all.

Not really. I know Andy, and he'd be good at this.
Really good.

> One of my friends at the meeting
> says her sister went to a place that did
> something called equine therapy. And it
> really helped her. They learned how to
> take care of horses, just normal stuff
> that you and I do all the time. But there
> isn't anything like that around here, so
> she can't keep doing it when she moves
> back home. I was thinking, wouldn't
> Sunny and Sam be good for that?

I chew my lip, remembering the way Sunny tosses
her head sometimes still when I get on her back.

> Well, maybe just Sam. Sunny could
> come around, though. You could train
> her. I could help.

I'm starting to ramble. I need to tell him my plan—
why have the sparrows started fluttering again?

So I think we should start an equine
therapy business. Mom could use her
accounting experience to manage it, you
and she could both train the horses, and
I could take care of them. Dad's such
a good teacher, I bet we could get him
to figure out the best way of planning
lessons or teaching anyone else who
wanted to learn more about it.

A whole notebook page gleams blue now, letters scrawled like rivers on every line.

This way Mom could have a job
again, and we wouldn't have to sell
Sunny and Sam.

I don't write the next thing, but it burns in
my mind: *And you would stop making the kinds
of mistakes that got you to Starshine Center in
the first place. No more hiding pills or strange
phones. You would make your own choices, but*

this time they'd be the right ones. It would be just like before.

I walk the letter to the mailbox in the dark so it will be ready to make its trip first thing in the morning.

CHAPTER 16

"Is it okay if I invite Mr. Hamilton over?" I ask Mom and Dad on Sunday afternoon. All week my head's been full of images that don't have anything to do with one another but are mashed together all the same: light slanting across Mr. Hamilton's barn, Sam startling at a wisp of tail in trees, Nari and her sister driving away in a pickup, their long hair streaming.

And my equine therapy plan. I keep waiting to hear back from Andy. Getting a yes from him will mean I can tell Mom and Dad all about it.

But Andy hasn't written back.

Mom looks up from the computer, where she's been scanning another job board. Dad has his lesson plan book open on his lap, but he's staring off into space instead of writing his usual notes.

They both shrug and say "Sure" at the same time. Then Mom asks, "Today?" And Dad asks, "Why?"

"Yes," I say to Mom, "if he can make it." Then I turn to Dad. "I need to ask him some more questions for my project."

That's not the whole reason, though. I'm also hoping I can convince Mr. Hamilton to come into the woods with me. He doesn't believe Jack's stories, but maybe seeing the horses will change his mind.

"Well, of course," Mom says. "Invite him over. I'll make coffee."

"I don't think we're really going to have enough time for that." The last thing I need is Mom taking up all of Mr. Hamilton's conversation time.

Mom snorts. "We don't need to spend light-years

at the table, Claire, but we do need to at least invite the man in."

She can't see me roll my eyes as I leave the room to call. And I don't feel a single flutter when I pick up my phone to dial Mr. Hamilton's number, or when I invite him over.

"No plans," Mr. Hamilton says when I ask. "How soon do you want me there?"

"The earlier the better." I want to leave enough time to find the wild horses.

His rough-sandpaper voice crackles. "I'll be right over."

It doesn't take long. The coffeepot beeps to tell us it's ready just as Mr. Hamilton's green pickup rolls down the driveway.

I go out to meet him, wrapping a sweater around my shoulders and slipping my boots on first. The air pierces my skin. Winter isn't far away anymore.

"Thanks for coming, Mr. Hamilton," I say as he opens the driver's-side door.

"My pleasure." Together, we walk inside.

"Glad to see you again, sir," Dad says, shaking hands. "Thanks again for helping Claire."

"I'm happy to," Mr. Hamilton says. "Good way to keep busy since my grandkids are so far away now. Claire actually reminds me of them."

"I can see that," Mom says. "And it's so nice to finally meet you. I remember Owen from school. Let me take your coat."

Once we're all sitting around the table, I explain what I want to find out and press RECORD on my phone's audio. "I learned so much from visiting you," I say. "But I'm interested in anything else you might remember about how people used horses on farms. Jack—I mean, your dad—maybe he told you stories?"

"He certainly did." Mr. Hamilton nods. "He loved talking about the old ways, especially since his parents stopped using horses. It's kind of funny that he missed them so much, seeing as how he was the one who got in the accident."

Mr. Hamilton explains that horses were crucial for logging, transporting wood down from mountains. Even though they were slower than the skidders that came later, they could wind around trees without much damage to the landscape. People rode behind on small wagons and attached the logs so they dragged on the ground.

"And sugaring was another matter," he says. "The horses would pull a large tank that had a little seat for the driver in front. They collected the buckets they'd already hung on the trees and poured sap into the tank."

"You know," Mom says, "my dad logged with horses for a while back when I was growing up. I don't remember it very well, though. Eventually he stopped and bought his wood instead."

"A lot of people have changed the old ways," says Mr. Hamilton. "The new ways do go a little faster. But still, horses can do just about anything, if you need them to."

I stop the recorder. "Would you like to meet ours?"

"Well, sure," Mr. Hamilton says quietly. "I haven't been near a horse since—well, since my grandkids left."

"Ours are really nice. I think you'll like them."

I can't look at Mom or Dad, or my voice will crack into pieces.

"We'll stay behind," Mom says, nodding toward her computer and Dad's chair with the lesson-plan book still open. "Claire can show you around the barn easily. She loves spending time there."

"It's my favorite place." I'm relieved that Mom and Dad aren't coming with us. If they'd both wanted to join, I wasn't sure what I was going to do.

"Our barn was always my favorite too," Mr. Hamilton says.

The sun's broken through the clouds and our walk to the barn is cold but bright. As soon as we step inside, Mr. Hamilton takes a deep breath and smiles. "Horses have a sweet smell, don't they?"

"I love it." I lead Sam out of his stall and put him in cross-ties so Mr. Hamilton can pet him, but he stands a bit to the side at first while I take out my brushes.

"You must have really liked horses, right?" I ask.

I already know the answer. Anybody who keeps horses has to love them, not just like them. It's like Dad says: They're a lot of work. A lot of money too.

Mr. Hamilton steps closer. "Yes. Growing up, I always thought our barn was perfect for horses, that it was a waste not to have them."

I laugh. "I thought that too, when I visited."

"I never managed to convince Dad, though," Mr. Hamilton says. "I guess he never really got over losing his team. He was scared to lose more."

I swallow hard. "I can kind of understand that. I can't imagine not having horses, but I also can't imagine having different ones. And actually...we aren't going to be able to keep Sunny and Sam."

"Oh, Claire, I'm so sorry to hear that," Mr. Hamilton says. "Why?"

My throat burns. Emptiness grows. But I keep my voice as strong as I can. "It's a lot of things. Mostly money. Horses are expensive, and our barn needs repairs."

"That's hard," Mr. Hamilton says quietly.

I start brushing flecks of hardened mud off Sam's coat. It's time to change the subject. "How did you get to be so good with horses if you didn't have them when you were growing up?"

"I hung around a lot with a friend down the road who kept them. Eventually I learned how to train and ended up getting the hang of it." Mr. Hamilton reaches out to stroke Sam's neck. "Ah. There's just something about being around them, isn't there? They always make me feel better."

"That's how Sunny and Sam help me," I say. "Sometimes I get this—feeling. In my chest. It's kind of like birds swoop in there and flutter around. It happens when I get nervous. But I never feel it when I'm working in the barn or riding."

"I know what you mean," Mr. Hamilton says. "And it doesn't surprise me at all that being with your horses helps."

Mr. Hamilton leads Sam back into his stall. The way he smiles gives me courage and I ask him what I really want to know: if he'll hike into the woods with me to find the wild horses, the ones I think are linked to Jack. I thought about riding, but I don't want Sunny to run away like she did before.

"I'm always glad to go hiking, but I hope I

didn't get you too excited about my dad's stories," Mr. Hamilton says. "He was so confused about that time in his life."

"The thing is, I think he was right," I say. "I've seen two wild horses already in the woods, and there's no way to explain where they came from."

"Wild horses?" Mr. Hamilton says, his voice a little less calm. "That's—interesting."

"Not everybody sees them," I say. "And I can tell that's not the only thing that's different about them. It feels like they're connected to Jack."

Mr. Hamilton raises his eyebrows. "Dad's horses couldn't still be alive. Even if they survived the fall into the water—which, remember, would be impossible—they'd have died long ago."

"I don't think they're the same horses. I just think they ended up there because of Jack some-how," I say. "It started with his horses, then whole generations grew up hiding in the forest. I've only seen two, but who knows how many there could be."

Mr. Hamilton pulls a cap out of his coat pocket and clears his throat. "You know what, I'm inter-ested. I'd like to see these wild horses."

In the quiet of the forest, Mr. Hamilton closes his eyes. I take deep breaths of cold fall air, the musty smell of dying maple leaves mixing with the spicy cedars that will keep growing all winter long. *Come on*, I think. *Show us where you are.*

Then I hear a snuffling in the trees behind us, the soft thud of a hoof sinking into dirt. A wisp of black tail disappears around a hemlock.

"Did you see that?" I ask.

"I'm not sure," Mr. Hamilton says. But he stands up and peers over to where the horse sprang away, and says, "Oh. This is interesting."

He holds up a horseshoe, rusted and flaking. It's so large, much too big for Sunny or Sam. They aren't draft horses—not like Jack's were. Not like these wild horses could be.

Mr. Hamilton gently hands me the horseshoe. "You might want to save that. Who knows how it got here—maybe from a logger, a long time ago."

"Or maybe it's from Jack's horses," I say. "Maybe it got buried here when they escaped."

Mr. Hamilton smiles. "Your imagination's about as impressive as Dad's."

"If we just wait a little longer, we'll see the horses again," I say. "They always come back."

Minutes pass. Two more times I swear I see a silver-dappled leg or back moving through the trees, and twice Mr. Hamilton says, "Maybe. Maybe you're right."

Then it's getting colder, and I know it's time to go. "Thanks for coming with me, Mr. Hamilton," I say. I can't hide my disappointment, but he puts a hand on my shoulder.

"Claire," he says. "It's true that I don't know what I saw. But that also means I'm not sure I *didn't* see what you think is there. Do you know the difference?"

My throat burns, and I can only nod instead of speaking.

"It will make even more sense as you get older," Mr. Hamilton says. "There will be so many situations you're not quite sure of. Eventually you realize that uncertainty is just part of the deal. And you do the best you can."

We leave the woods in silence, the horseshoe dangling from my fingers.

After Mr. Hamilton drives away, I tell Mom and Dad I'm going back to the barn to finish up with a few chores.

But that's not the whole truth.

Mr. Hamilton said it was hard to be sure about everything in life, but if I can get a closer look at the ring of stones by the lake, I can figure out if it is what I think it is: the opening to a tunnel. I think Jack was right—the items from the box came from Pine Lake. And the horses *did* fall through Cedar Lake. They just found their way from one to the other, and a tunnel would explain how. I saddle Sam quickly.

As we head into the woods, I take a deep breath, letting the cold, clean smells of late fall fill my nose. The sunlight's fading, though, the sky overhead the color of a bruise. I don't have much time.

Sam almost seems used to the dappled horses now. As they curl through the tree trunks, their hoofprints landing softly, he just nods and snuffles.

And they seem to know exactly where we need to go, because they stay a few steps ahead, pressing up the path until we reach the woods and the border with state land that leads to the lake.

A text pings, and I pull out my phone. It's Mom.

> **Where are you?**

Oh no. I never texted to tell her I was heading out.

> **Finishing up chores.**

Hopefully Mom isn't out at the barn to catch me in a lie.

> **OK. But come back soon. It's getting dark.**

Whew. She must still be at the house. But still, this is risky.

Sam and I pick our way past branches until we reach a small clearing, just before the trees thicken and cluster close to the water. I don't have time or light to figure out the best route with him, so I pull a halter over Sam's head and loop the lead rope I brought around a sturdy low-hanging branch.

It's important not to tie it tight—even with calm, steady Sam, I wouldn't risk having him startle and pull himself into a trap. Horses have died that way.

"Stay here, buddy," I whisper. It's getting darker. I look past my shoulder and just barely see the horses waiting in the distance, their sides lifting in and out as they breathe. In the fading light their dappled bodies seem transparent and soft as fog, but solid too. Then I walk toward the lake.

The ring of stones is still there, stacked and layered, held in place like a black waterfall laced with silver. I edge as close as I can to the water without stepping into it. Now I'm near enough to touch one of the stones, and I do, feeling its cold, smooth surface. I reach one foot out to a strip of sand jutting past the rock and balance on that, my other foot squarely planted on the bank. From there I can peer into the space between the stones, where darkness gathers.

As I look into it, blinking, my eyes slowly adjust.

I turn on my phone's flashlight to be sure, and it's exactly what I thought. Packed sand lines the bottom, making a path. The top is bound close with the stretching, thickly woven roots of trees. And the sides are covered with stones.

I can't tell how far back it goes. I can't tell where it leads. But if Cedar Lake is at the other end, it's not hard to imagine weary horses sinking down, then finding a hidden path beyond the frozen water, a way out when everyone thought there couldn't be.

It's not hard to imagine the horses ending up right here.

Even though the tunnel is set back into the bank, even though it's masked by trees that bend so close to the water that they freeze into the ice when winter comes, I can't believe I've never seen it. Because looking at it now, some small and secret part of me feels that I've always known it was here.

CHAPTER 17

"Dinner!" Dad calls from downstairs. I was going to wait to talk with Mom and Dad about my equine therapy plan until I got a response from Andy, but hearing Mr. Hamilton's words about uncertainty makes me think I should keep going after all. The sooner we get started, the better we'll all be.

Dad slides a pan of lasagna out of the oven while Mom fills water glasses. I set plates and napkins on the table while the sparrows inside me cluster and swirl. Once we've all sat down and

Dad's sliced big helpings for all of us, I take a deep breath and start.

"I have an idea." I cut my fork into melty cheese, watching the silver handle catch light from the overhead lamp. "I already wrote Andy about it, but I haven't heard back."

"Oh yeah?" Mom asks. Dad looks up. The air hangs heavy with their waiting.

Seeing their eyes change as I tell them about Nari and her sister, about equine therapy, and about my plan for Andy and our family feels like watching clouds shift over the mountains. When I'm done, they look at each other, then back at me.

"Wow," Mom says. "Honey, that's"—she looks at Dad again, but he's leaning back in his chair, his arms crossed, staring at the ceiling like he does when he's thinking hard—"definitely not what I expected you to say. Not at all. I'm shocked actually. But..." She clasps her hands under her chin and looks at me, her forehead all wrinkly like she's trying to figure me out. "I'm also impressed."

Pride pushes the sparrows away and they close their eyes to sleep under its warm glow.

"Can you tell me a little more about this equine therapy, though?" Mom asks. "I know you said it can help people who are struggling with addiction and other issues. But how, exactly?"

"Working with animals has been proven to be therapeutic," I say. "Like, with scientific studies. I've done a lot of research on it, for my project."

"This is part of your history project too?" Mom asks. "How interesting."

"We're supposed to connect history to the present anyway," I explain. "And this is something people still use horses for. We could set up a program where people would make regular appointments. We could teach them how to take care of the horses, even the really basic stuff, and then how to ride."

"Would these be private appointments?" Mom asks. "Or would people come in groups?"

"I think we could do either one eventually," I say. "But at first I would want to do private appointments, so people could really develop a relationship with our horses."

"You've thought this through." Mom's eyes gleam.

But Dad's looking at me differently, and I can't quite figure it out. In a way it feels like he's seeing me as another grown-up. But in another way, it feels like my idea's on the other side of a window he's about to slam shut.

I wish he would say something. But he stays quiet, so I fill the empty space with more words.

"When people work with horses," I say, "it helps them see themselves more clearly. It makes them feel better."

Mom squeezes my shoulder. "Does it do that for you too?"

Inside, the sparrows rustle. I've never totally explained to my parents how it feels to have them swoop inside the way I explained it to Mr. Hamilton.

"When I'm nervous about something, it always goes away when I'm with Sunny and Sam," I say. Maybe that's enough for now.

"Sometimes making a leap isn't such a bad idea," Dad says, clearing his throat. "The job market hasn't exactly been promising." He keeps his voice soft, puts his hand on Mom's.

"So are you guys saying yes? We could keep Sunny and Sam, and open the business, and—"

A smile tugs at Mom's lips, but Dad shakes his head and looks at her. When he speaks, his voice has that harder edge I heard in the truck.

"Not necessarily," he says. "We need to think logically about how wise it would be to involve Andy in a business plan like this. June, you couldn't do all the management and accounting, *plus* all the training. Andy would need to be a pretty big piece of this puzzle."

"But that's the point," I say. "I know he would want to. He could help a lot."

Dad sighs. "Andy hasn't been exactly—reliable. Not lately."

But I don't want them to start talking about why Andy could make things harder. I want to picture him reading my letter and pushing his baseball cap back on his head and scratching behind his ears and writing me back to say *I'm in, Little C.*

We should be talking about details.

"There'd be other startup costs too, and then ongoing ones," Mom says. "I'm sure there'd be changes we'd have to make to the ring, supplies we'd need, certification, insurance issues—those all take money." She doesn't say *that we don't have*. I know it's what she's thinking.

But Mom doesn't know about the certification program I researched, or the five hundred dollars that would help pay for it if my History Fair presentation is good enough to win. Thinking about how disappointed she'd be to know about the prize money and then to watch me not get it sends the sparrows spinning in circles, so I keep this one little thing to myself.

Still, Mom's voice is sun-bright and clear. She's moving her hands while she talks now, and I think for a second she'll jump out of her seat. "I could really put all those skills from the office to use," she says. "And what a great cause. What a way to give back, now that Andy's almost better."

Dad looks at her carefully. "June," he says, "we've talked about this specific issue already. It's not like there's going to be one moment when Andy's problems are over."

"You're not thinking of *him* when you say

that," Mom says, shaking her head. "He isn't just anybody. He's Andy!"

Dad sighs. "We'd be taking a risk."

"Oh, George," Mom says, shaking her head. "You don't need to be so cynical about that. He's our son."

"It's not cynicism. It's realism." Dad takes a bite of lasagna, chews, swallows. Puts his fork down. He's using his teacher voice, which is calm but firm, smooth as stone. "It's like you're forgetting—" But then he stops as Mom whips her head around, her eyes burning, her mouth frozen.

I wait for him to finish the sentence. *Forgetting what?*

But nobody says anything. Mom shakes her head, Dad says, "Never mind," and they both go back to chewing lasagna like nothing happened at all.

In school on Monday, Maya has her Edna Beard notes perfectly arranged: graphic organizers printed, annotated articles cataloged in a binder with tabs marking dates and topics, plus labeled folders in her Google Drive with pages full of notes and a working bibliography. But she's been staring out the window a lot today, and I've seen Ms. Larkin's eyes dart toward her.

"Hey," I say. "Do you want to come over later?"

Maya shifts her eyes from the binder to me. "I don't know if I can."

That doesn't make sense. Maya's parents would let her—they always do. I keep trying. "I'll come to your house, then."

"Don't you have your support group meeting tonight?" Maya twists her hands in her lap.

"Yeah," I say. "But that's like, way later. My parents can pick me up in time."

"Um, okay," she says, which is the weirdest thing. Maya's usually a lot more excited to hang out.

But Ms. Larkin's already at our table, so I'll have to put off figuring out what's going on with Maya.

"There's a ton of information." I pull up my Google Drive and show her the folder marked

Article Notes. "And it turns out some of the ways people used to use horses can still be helpful now. For example, logging with horses can be better for the forests, because horses have less impact on the trees. That means they don't destroy the woods as much as machines do."

"Wow, Claire," Ms. Larkin says. "You've done a lot of work since we last checked in. Are you focusing your connection to the present on how people can still use horses the way they used to?"

"Actually, I'm looking at both: how people can use horses in ways that are similar to the past, and also how people use them for new jobs," I say. "Like equine therapy. It works in lots of situations, for people who have physical disabilities or problems like depression. It's something a machine can't ever do."

"I've heard of equine therapy," Ms. Larkin says. "It's very relevant. Was Mr. Hamilton helpful at all, as a primary source?"

"Yes," I say quietly. "He was really helpful." *And not just in the ways you'd expect*, I think.

Ms. Larkin moves over to Maya, who opens her

binder and points to a few new notes, but as she explains her latest research, I notice her words aren't tumbling and tripping over each other like they usually do. I hear the murmurs of Ms. Larkin's gentle questions and Maya's mechanical responses—I even see her shrug at one point, which is definitely *not* Maya. Maya would never shrug about Edna Beard. As she stands up, Ms. Larkin places a hand on Maya's shoulder. "Let me know if you need anything else," she says as she moves on to the next table.

CHAPTER 18

At Maya's house, familiar, comforting smells of chile and cumin waft from the kitchen. Ms. Gonzalez is already home, which seems strange. She's a nurse and usually has to work late on Mondays.

"Hola, nena." Ms. Gonzalez wraps her arms around Maya. "Claire, it's good to see you." She hugs me next, gripping tight. Ms. Gonzalez always gives the best hugs, warm and strong and lasting just long enough to convince you everything will be okay. "I just pulled out a pan of enchiladas.

Thought it would be good to have dinner all set before our doctor's appointment."

"How's Papi?" Maya asks.

"Resting in his office," Ms. Gonzalez says. "But you can go see him for sure." She checks her watch. "We just have to leave for the appointment in about fifteen minutes."

That explains why she's home so early.

Maya starts toward the office, but I stand still, not sure if I should follow.

"Come on," Maya says.

Slowly, she pushes the door open. "Papi?"

The room is dark and cool. Mr. Gonzalez loves plants, and he keeps pots of them on nearly every surface. But today's late-afternoon light can't push through the pulled-shut blinds.

I see him lying on the couch where Maya and I used to bring our dolls and have tea parties. He never seemed to mind us being there. He'd just keep working with headphones on, tuning out our noise but turning to smile at us or give us pepper-mints every once in a while.

Now Mr. Gonzalez opens his eyes. "Mija," he

says. "Oh, and Claire! Hello. How nice to see you."
His voice sounds tired, worn.

"It's nice to see you too, Mr. Gonzalez." I want
to shake his hand, but I also feel like I should stand
outside the bubble that seems to surround him, a
bubble that's fragile enough to burst.

"How are you feeling, Papi?" Maya asks. She
sits on the edge of the couch.

"You know me." He gives her a thumbs-up.
"Thinking about training for a triathlon, actually.
You in?"

Maya makes a sound that's sort of like a laugh,
but it has something else behind it.

"Seriously, mija," he says. "I'm fine." He pushes
up to a sitting position and squeezes Maya around
the shoulders. "How's that project coming?"

"It's okay," Maya says. Her eyes search her
dad's face. "I started designing my slideshow. And
I'm making a costume."

"Good, good," Mr. Gonzalez says. He closes
his eyes briefly, presses one hand to his forehead.
"That's really good."

I see what Maya means. Her dad would usually

ask more questions, give tips, or pull up interest-ing websites on his computer. Now all he can say is "good." But it's obvious that he's trying, that the one word is as much as he can manage.

"Claire," he says. "How's your brother?"

Maya flinches a little. It's such a small move-ment, most people wouldn't notice, but I do.

"He likes Starshine," I say.

Mr. Gonzalez's eyes hold mine steady. "I'm glad to hear that."

"Yeah," I say. "But it will be good to have him home. Hopefully soon."

He leans back against the couch. "I wish him the best," he says quietly.

Maya stares at the floor.

Then there's a soft knock, and Ms. Gonzalez comes in. "Sorry to break up the party, but it's time for us to head out."

"Ladies, my dance card is full." Mr. Gonza-lez's voice wavers, but he gives us the same smile I remember from when I was little. Ms. Gonzalez holds out an arm and he takes it, slowly standing up and moving with careful steps to the door.

When they leave, there's silence.

Maya shakes her head and picks at her shoe-laces. When she finally looks at me, I can see in her face the weight of something she doesn't want to say. I can feel the words coming, like snow starting overnight, thick and quiet in the dark.

"Wow," I start. "It seems like—"

"I need to talk to you about something," Maya says.

I close my mouth, startled. She never interrupts.

"You'll be mad at first," she says, her voice wavery. "But"—she takes a deep breath—"then I know you'll understand."

Sparrows soar through the windows, hover at my shoulders. I'm not supposed to get this feeling with Maya, but it's unmistakable: the rustle of wings, the flutter in my chest.

"You know how my dad's been really—hard to talk to lately. Like, hasn't been interested in my project, goes into his office and shuts the door as soon as he gets home from work, has to go to the doctor." Maya looks toward the door. "I mean, you saw it for yourself."

"I know." I don't say anything else. I just want her to keep going so that whatever she's going to say can be out there. Done. Ready to deal with. It's so much worse when it's hiding in the shadows.

"Well, the doctors say he has cardiomyopathy, which happens because of stress. Which my mom says he gets way too much of at work. He has so many tough cases." Maya covers her eyes with one hand. The next thing she says is so quiet I can barely hear it. "Cases like Andy's."

The sparrows dive down in a single rush of heavy wings.

"Wait," I say. "What? Why would Andy have to see your dad? He wasn't a 'case.'"

Maya takes a deep breath. "That's the thing, Claire," she says. "He actually was."

"Why would Andy have to go to court?" I wonder if my voice sounds as shaky as I feel. "All he did was take too many pain pills. He was *hurt*, Maya. He needed them. It just…" I catch Maya's eyes, holding mine steady. Not blinking. "It just went too far."

"That's not all he did, Claire," Maya says, a

little louder now. "He wasn't just taking pills himself. He was selling them to other people."

That hot, sharp feeling I got in Mr. Hamilton's barn is coming back. It's like a flame, and Maya's words are little puffs of air making it grow.

I shake my head. "No, he wasn't." But images of the pill bottles in the closet, the cell phone with the strange numbers, swim in my mind. I shut my eyes to squeeze them out. "No!"

The sparrows' wings are fluttering so loudly, I barely hear what Maya says next. "I'm sorry, Claire."

"How do you even know this stuff?" I ask. "And why didn't you tell me before?"

Maya's eyes fill with tears. "I wanted to, at first. I overheard my parents talking about it one night when they thought I was asleep, and I made them tell me. But they said your parents should be the ones to discuss it with you, not me. Besides, I could see how upset you were about Andy and I just thought—it wasn't the right time."

"It would never be the right time." My voice feels icy. But Maya does have a point—if this is even true, I have no idea why my parents didn't tell me about it. They should have.

"Papi said it was one small example of hard things he has to deal with every day." Maya takes a deep breath. "He said he always tries to do his best, but sometimes the choices are really difficult. Like, it's also because of him that Andy went to the rehab center."

I shake my head. This is so confusing. "*Andy* decided to go. Even he told me that."

"Well, that's sort of true," Maya says. "Papi didn't actually *force* Andy, but he basically made it the best option. Andy picked Starshine Center because if he hadn't gone there, he would have had to go to jail."

"Jail?" My voice sounds like someone else's. Angry.

"Wait a second. The point here is that Andy had options." Now Maya's eyes seem to be on fire. "It was actually really nice of Papi to give a choice. Can't you see that?"

"*Nice* of him? That's not much of a choice at all!"

"Oh my gosh, Claire," Maya says. "Hello!

Dealing drugs is illegal, remember? Look, I know how much you miss Andy." She holds up her hands. "But this is probably good, you know? Maybe he kind of needed—a wake-up call."

"No!" My voice cuts the air. All my happy memories of Mr. Gonzalez—all the ice creams and trips to his office and barbecues on the beach— they scatter away. "That was really dumb of your dad, Maya. It screwed up our family."

Maya's eyes narrow. "My dad did not screw up your family. He works really hard for people like Andy," she says, her voice cold as gusts of wind. "It makes him stressed, trying to figure out how to do the right thing all the time without hurting anyone. You think I'm happy about the fact that he couldn't even go over my Edna Beard presentation because he was up so late in his office, working instead of sleeping?"

"Who cares about Edna Beard!" My face heats up. *People like Andy?* At this exact moment, I wonder if I actually know Maya at all.

"My project is just one tiny example of why work is a problem for him!" Maya yells. "Here's another one! The doctor told my dad to take a medical leave because he's worried he might have a *heart attack*. This isn't a joke!"

Nari's voice comes through clear. She said her sister was "the coolest person."

So is Andy.

Nari's sister also made big mistakes.

So did Andy.

Sparrows whirl in circles. I don't know how to feel.

But I do know that even though Andy started acting different before he left home, being at Starshine has just made him even more different. Now he might not even *want* to come home. And now I also know why he had to leave.

"Papi was trying to help, Claire." Maya's voice is calm on the surface, but I hear a storm gathering underneath. "Because that's what Andy needs. *Help*. There's nothing wrong with that, you know. Everybody has problems. You can't pretend Andy doesn't, just like you can't pretend my dad will definitely be okay. The truth is, you don't know."

Her eyes soften a bit, but the words gathering inside me pierce like sticks, and I throw them at her.

"Andy would have been fine!" I yell. "He would have figured it out. He didn't need Starshine. And if he hadn't gone there, Mom and Dad wouldn't be paying so much money for it. Did you know that's partly why they want to sell Sunny and Sam?"

I realize my hands are shaking. I don't like thinking about whether Mom and Dad would still want to sell Sunny and Sam if Andy hadn't gone to Starshine. I don't want him to be the reason I lose them.

"You know I'm sad about the horses too." Maya shakes her head. She's quieter now. Calmness has come back into her voice and it only makes my sparrows fight harder. "But Andy messed up. I feel bad that he got a back injury; that wasn't fair. But he got addicted to pain pills and then he started selling them. That means he was hurting other people too, not only himself."

I stand up, pull my phone out. My hand trembles when I hit CONTACTS and I barely recognize my own voice when I finally speak. "Yeah, Mom, can you pick me up? Maya's parents are busy...five minutes is perfect."

"Ask your parents how Andy got the money for his pills," she says. "Then maybe you'll understand."

I open the office door. The room around me feels like a ship, pitching and heaving in storms.

I stumble down the hall, taking big gulps of air to make the sparrows leave.

But they stay. They're whirling too fast for me to catch, their wings slapping my ribs.

No matter how hard I try to brush the sound of Maya's voice away, it's the only thing I can hear.

CHAPTER 19

Maya didn't mean anything. That's what I tell myself. She's scared for her dad, and the flame inside her just grew too big and started burning everything else it touched—like me.

She'll text me later and tell me it was nothing. All made up.

But the pills in the closet. The phone. *Ask your parents how Andy got the money...*

I push Maya's front door open, and as soon as I make it outside, sink to the ground, knees up, fists pressed to my eyes, I put both hands on my chest. *Breathe in, out.*

It takes a long time, but finally the sparrows leave. There were so many more of them this time, more than I could count. Flocks and flocks, burrowing deep inside.

I stand up. Suddenly I realize my lips are dry, my tongue thick, my hands quivering like drifting leaves. I lick my lips, wish for a water bottle. Mom always has one in the car.

By the time she pulls up, my hands have stopped shaking. When I slide into the front seat and grab the water bottle from the cup holder, drinking long and slow, Mom glances my way.

"You're awfully quiet," she says.

Inside I'm blazing fire. Roaring. Mom just can't hear it.

"How's Maya?" she asks, her eyes flitting between the road and me.

If I open my mouth to speak, flames will surge out and burn both of us. But if I don't, Mom will keep talking. And I need quiet.

"She's fine," I manage. Then I look out the window. The trees are so much barer now. Bouquets of leaves have browned and tumbled away, leaving skeletons behind. I breathe quietly, trying to steady the wings inside.

Watching the trees helps. I focus on each one as we slide past. By the time we reach the community center, the flutters are gone, but there's an empty stillness inside me.

Once I'm at the meeting, I manage to say "Hey" to Nari as I sit next to her, and wave at Caleb and Anna across the room. Marcus comes in a little late, just as Sharon's getting started, and I smile at him. But inside I'm still a shell. I try to turn the sounds in the room into words and the words into something I can understand.

Sharon's voice finally pushes through my emptiness. *Honesty*. That's what she's talking about now.

"Addicts are asked to be honest with themselves," she's saying. "But we need to be honest with ourselves too. Seeing situations clearly isn't easy, but it's the only way to move forward. It's the only way to grow."

My eyes burn. I blink back tears.

When Sharon opens the meeting for sharing, I surprise myself.

"I don't usually like talking, especially to a group of people," I say. "But something happened."

I feel Nari's eyes on me. I see Anna nod, encouraging me to keep going.

"My brother Andy's been in rehab because he got addicted to pain pills. He had a really bad injury. The pills took his pain away, you know? So I understand it, in a way. I mean, I know it's not *good*, but it also makes some sense." I take a deep, shaky breath, then explain about Nate and the textbook, and the pills and phone in Andy's closet. "I knew it was weird, when Nate came by. I knew something was off. But I didn't want to think about it."

The more I talk, the stronger my voice sounds. For such a long time I didn't want to tell anybody here my story. I didn't think they'd understand. Now I want to say everything. I explain Maya's secret, her dad's illness, Andy's case.

"I really didn't want to believe her. I still don't. How could my brother bring his problem to other people? None of you know Andy, but trust me, he's an amazing person." My throat swells. My eyes water. But nobody here looks surprised. They know exactly what I mean.

"I thought—'This isn't him,'" I say. "I mean, it *is* him. It's part of him. But it can't be all of him. That's why it doesn't make any sense."

I stop talking, and silence fills the room. It's not the bare, lonely kind of silence that makes you feel like nobody's listening. It's the full, warm kind that happens when everybody's reaching out to you with their eyes and leaning forward in their chairs and they're all thinking the same thing so hard that the words somehow find you and tell you: *It's okay. When you're ready to say more, we'll be here.*

"None of our stories make sense," I say. "Because none of these people deserve to have addiction. Anna's mom loves her, and Nari's sister is supercool, and Marcus's dad is probably trying his best even though I think he needs to do a lot better at showing it. The stories don't make sense, but they're also real. I want things to be easier but they just aren't. It doesn't mean I can't be strong anyway."

I look at Nari, and she's smiling, her eyes glimmering.

And then the truth blooms inside me, and even though it's not what I want to see, just having it there feels right somehow.

"I think about those pills, and that phone, and I know my friend is right," I say. "Trying to pretend she isn't is pointless. What I really need to figure out is what to do now."

I stop talking, but everyone still waits, giving me a chance to say anything else I might need. "That's all," I say quietly, and the chorus of "Thanks, Claire," makes me feel better than I thought it would.

After the meeting, we hang out a little longer at the cookie table.

"Honesty is a huge step, Claire," Sharon says. "I'm proud of you for taking it. And for sharing. We love having your voice in the circle."

"It wasn't actually that bad," I say.

"Yeah, I guess we aren't *totally* scary," Anna says, punching me lightly on the arm. "When you said something about those pills before, I kind of realized what might be going on."

"So did I," Marcus says. "But it seemed like you would figure it out for yourself."

"Yeah." Nari nods. "And you did."

Hearing Nari's voice makes a question that's been bubbling inside since I talked to Mom and Dad spill over. "Nari, I don't understand why your sister had to go to jail," I say. "Andy had a choice."

Hurt passes over Nari's face, a skittering cloud. "I know," she says. "Pia didn't, even though she ended up going to rehab too. It's not fair."

"The system often isn't fair," Sharon says, her voice soft but firm. "It usually skews against people of color, who often face jail time in cases where a white person wouldn't."

Heat rushes to my face. "But Andy's judge—he wouldn't have been like that," I say.

"It's not about one judge," Sharon says. "Nari's in a different district and her sister probably didn't see the same one. But either way, this is a wide-spread social issue—bigger than a single case."

Sharon's words expand inside me, pushing against the edges of what I thought I knew. They're uncomfortable, but I know they need to be there.

"It's true," Nari says. "I really like what you shared, though, Claire. Because I do feel like I'm strong. I feel like we all are."

"Kind of seems impossible some days," Caleb says, frowning.

"But then sometimes it just gets better too," Nari says quietly. "When you're least expecting it."

"Having a thing that's *yours* helps," Sharon says. "Remember when we talked about that? Giving yourself what you need is also the best way to help someone else. Keep that in mind this week, okay?"

We all nod and grab extra cookies, then start heading out.

"Hey, Claire," Anna says. "We should exchange numbers."

"Yeah," says Marcus, and Caleb takes out his phone too.

We send texts and pretty soon I have three more contacts, not counting Nari. I have to bite the insides of my cheeks to keep my smile from spreading across my whole face.

Before Nari heads downtown, she turns to me. "Thanks again for having me over," she says. "Working with your horse ended up being a lot more fun than I thought it would be. And honestly? It helped me think about my sister differently too."

"Really?" I ask. "Like how?"

"I don't exactly know. Maybe part of it was doing something she had done, and realizing that when she first started working with horses, she probably felt a lot of the same feelings I did," Nari says. "I just thought—well, she's still herself. And knowing she likes the horses so much now even though she was probably scared before…it made me think she can change in good ways too. Other people have, so why not her?"

I swallow hard. Knowing more about Andy has turned my feelings about him upside down, but what Nari says makes a lot of sense.

"I know my parents are right," Nari continues.

"We are still a family and we can support each other. I can be there for my sister and still do the kinds of things Sharon talks about, like letting go and stuff."

"Sharon's definitely got her checklist going," I say. "But it seems not so bad."

Nari laughs. "As checklists go. Anyway, I would love to come over again and learn more about horses, if that works for you."

"That would be so cool." My mind starts racing forward, filling with future rides in the woods. But then the race stops short, and I remember: I don't know how much longer I'll have horses. The equine therapy plan depends on Andy, and I don't know what he'll say. Or what I even want him to say.

Nari must see my face change. "It would be fun to just hang out too, though," she says. "With or without Sam."

"Definitely." Mom's car pulls up, and I wave goodbye before sliding in, still thinking about the new numbers in my phone and plans with Nari.

"Good meeting?" Mom asks.

"Actually, yeah." But I turn away from her,

look out the window. Part of me doesn't want to talk to Mom, but the rest of me wants to hurl enough words at her and Dad to bury them knee-deep, until they can explain why they hid the truth about Andy from me.

"That's great," Mom says. "You seem to be enjoying them more."

I watch the mountains roll past, the same shapes as always, but with different colors. Inside me, words gather like storm clouds.

At home, Mom stops by the mailbox, leans out the window to retrieve a stack of envelopes. "Oh," she says as she shuffles through bills. "Looks like Andy wrote you back."

A sparrow drops the envelope in my hands, flutters into my heart as Mom continues down the driveway. "You're not going to open it?" she asks.

I shake my head, try to keep my voice steady. "Not yet."

Inside, Dad's taking a chicken out of the oven. Mom opens the fridge, starts assembling salad ingredients. I kick my boots off on the porch and stomp into the kitchen.

"Wow, Claire," Dad says. "What an entrance."

I can't keep the words inside anymore. The car ride was long enough.

"I know about Andy," I say, my voice heavy.

Mom whips around, her eyes wide. "What? Claire, we were just in the car together. You didn't—"

"I know about the pills," I say. "And about Mr. Gonzalez basically making Andy go to Starshine."

Mom's eyes widen. "Who told you that, honey?"

"Maya," I say. "She said Andy deserved it. I was really mad at her. Now I'm not really sure who to be mad at. Why did you guys lie to me?"

Dad sighs, closes his eyes. "It was a mistake, Claire. We should have told you."

So it's true. It's definitely true.

"We wanted to protect you," Mom says quietly. "We thought you didn't need to know the full extent of what Andy had done."

"He's my brother!" I yell. "Don't you think I would've found out eventually?"

Mom pinches her lips together. "We didn't think it through carefully enough, but there's nothing to worry about now. We got rid of the pills, and Andy's at Starshine. He'll get better there."

Her words punch right in my stomach, and I feel the breath go out of me in a single rush. "Getting better takes a long time. And you didn't get rid of all the pills."

Dad's eyes search mine: cloudy, confused.

Mom blinks, shakes her head. "What do you mean?"

"I found more of them in his closet," I say. "Plus a weird phone."

Mom and Dad look like statues, frozen in place. Finally, Mom speaks. "Can you show us?"

I lead them up the steps, my heart pounding, then burst into Andy's room, not tiptoeing this time. For one second, I think I might have imagined the pills, that when I reach under the quilts and into the Secret Pillow they won't be there anymore. But they are.

"Wow," Dad says. "Okay. We missed those."

"We checked his closet, though," Mom says.

"Remember? I used a step stool so I could see that top shelf."

"These were in the back corner, where we used to make forts," I explain. "In the Secret Pillow."

"Secret Pillow?" Mom and Dad both say, scrunching their eyebrows.

"Never mind." I shake my head. "What I don't understand is how Andy got so many pills in the first place. Did the doctor prescribe him, like, ten million bottles at once?"

Dad shakes his head. "Well, there's something else you should know," he says. Then he turns to Mom. "What's the point in hiding things from her anymore?"

Mom presses her hands to her forehead.

"Know what?" Fire rages inside my brain. I can barely see.

Dad clears his throat and looks at me. "Claire, your brother stole money from us."

"It was just once!" Mom says. "There's no need to exaggerate."

The room spins. Maya's words come rushing

back: *Ask your parents how Andy got the money for his pills.*

"It was not just once," Dad says, shaking his head at Mom. "You know it was multiple times, over the course of several weeks." Then he looks back at me. "Claire, this will be hard to hear, but Andy took quite a bit of cash from your mother's purse and used it to buy pills from various sources. Your mother and I spoke to him about it, and it seemed to stop. But Andy didn't get better. Do you remember?"

My eyes fill. I don't like remembering how Andy acted in those weeks leading up to Starshine: how he never seemed to have time to hike up Pebble Mountain anymore, how he always seemed tired, how he'd move in and out of the house like a shadow.

"That's when we decided to search his room, and realized he had started selling pills to other people," Dad says.

I wipe my eyes. Breathe.

"Maya's dad isn't the real reason Andy ended up at Starshine, Claire," Mom says. "We are."

Her lip trembles, and Dad puts his hand on her

shoulder. *"Andy's* the reason Andy ended up at Starshine, June," he says softly.

I hear the wings, high overhead, fluttering closer. I try to breathe, but there's no air anymore.

"Fine," Mom says. "But we brought the pills to the police. We told them what happened, and then the court date was set."

Sparrows sweep in swiftly, rush through my heart, carry every bit of it away.

"And you never told me." My voice echoes, empty, like it's coming from outside me.

"We did plan to tell you at some point," Dad says. "But time passed, and we let it. That was a mistake."

Mom nods. "You deserved to know what was going on," she says. "Now that you do, we can think about where to go from here. Andy's been doing well at Starshine."

"But we still need to be cautious." Dad reaches for her hand and squeezes it.

"And supportive," Mom says. "Don't forget that. If Andy can help with equine therapy, we should really consider it."

Dad sighs. "We will," he says, "though of course, we'd still need to discuss finances."

But I barely hear them. My eyes are open now. I'm already stepping back into my boots.

"Claire," I hear Dad say. "Let's all sit down. We can talk more over dinner." But I open the door.

"Where are you going?" Mom asks, her voice far away. I let the door swing closed behind me.

Inside, the hot flame I felt before grows. Except now when I think about who kindled it, I see Andy's face.

How could he do this to our family?

CHAPTER 20

In the barn, I tear the envelope clumsily, leaving a jagged rip and sending little bits of paper floating to the ground.

> DEAR LITTLE C.,
>
> HEY, I'LL SKIP THE JOKE THIS TIME. I COULD TELL
> YOUR LETTER WAS PRETTY SERIOUS STUFF.

I frown. Andy without a joke doesn't sound right. But I keep reading, my eyes trying to take the whole letter in at once without missing anything.

It's all there, in black and white.

THIS SCHOOL PROJECT SOUNDS PRETTY COOL.
YOU'VE BEEN WORKING HARD, WHICH IS EXACTLY WHAT
I EXPECT FROM MY LITTLE SIS. KEEP IT UP, OKAY?

EQUINE THERAPY? I GUESS I'VE NEVER HEARD
OF IT BEFORE, TECHNICALLY, BUT PRETTY SURE
TAKING CARE OF SUNNY AND SAM COUNTS. SO I
GUESS YOU AND I GET IT FOR FREE. WELL, NOT
FOR FREE, BUT YOU KNOW WHAT I MEAN. IT SOUNDS
COOL TO DO IT FOR OTHER PEOPLE TOO. YOU'D BE
GREAT AT IT.

YOU SHOULD BE ABLE TO KEEP SUNNY AND SAM.
AND LEAVE IT TO YOU TO COME UP WITH A SUPERSMART
WAY TO DO IT!

BUT LC, I CAN'T DO WHAT YOU'RE ASKING ME TO
DO. I CAN'T BE THE TRAINER.

My eyes blur. I reread the line. What does Andy
mean, he *can't* be the trainer? He's an even better
trainer than Mom—she always says so. He went
beyond everything she taught him.

BEING HERE AT STARSHINE HAS MADE ME THINK
THROUGH A LOT OF STUFF. LIKE WHO I AM, AND WHERE
I'M HEADED, AND WHAT I WANT TO DO WITH THE REST
OF MY LIFE. SOUNDS INTENSE, I KNOW. BUT WHAT AM I
GONNA DO HERE EXCEPT THINK?

He added a smiley face there: sideways nose,
high eyebrows. If I close my eyes, I can see his
crooked smile.

I THOUGHT ABOUT WHAT YOU SAID. I REALLY DID.
BUT I DON'T WANT TO LIVE AT HOME WHEN I LEAVE
STARSHINE. I TURNED EIGHTEEN NOT LONG AFTER I
LEFT HOME, REMEMBER? I'VE GOT TO GET OUT ON MY
OWN. BESIDES, I TOLD YOU I REALLY WANT TO BE AN
AGRICULTURAL MECHANIC.

I can't believe what I'm reading. The hot, sharp
flame grows.

THIS BOX YOU FOUND SOUNDS PRETTY COOL! YOU'LL
HAVE TO SHOW IT TO ME. IT'S STILL HARD TO BELIEVE

ALL THAT STUFF ABOUT THE HORSES AND THE TUNNEL UNDER THE LAKES, THOUGH. ARE YOU SURE YOU SAW THIS STUFF? LIKE IT WASN'T YOUR IMAGINATION? IT SOUNDS AWESOME BUT KIND OF WEIRD TOO?

ANYWAY, I REALLY WANT TO SEE THAT STONE YOU FOUND IN THE BOX. IN OUR GROUP MEETINGS, THEY PASS AROUND A BASKET OF THESE SMOOTH POLISHED STONES. THEY CALL THEM "WORRY STONES," I GUESS BECAUSE YOU CAN SORT OF RUB YOUR WORRIES OUT OF YOURSELF AND INTO THEM. WE GET TO HOLD ON TO THEM WHILE EVERYONE'S TALKING.

DOESN'T SOUND LIKE MUCH, BUT I REALLY LIKE THE STONES. WHEN I HAVE ONE IN MY HAND, IT HELPS ME THINK. AND IT MAKES ME CALM. SO SAVE THAT STONE, WOULD YOU? I DON'T THINK I'LL GET TO TAKE THESE ONES WITH ME WHEN I LEAVE.

LOVE,
ANDY

My eyes blur and I press my palms into them. Sniffle into my sleeve. Andy's words feel like a tall, thick door that just latched shut.

He doesn't believe me. He's not going to help us. He's on his own path.

But so am I.

Memories of the Andy I knew—Andy cupping his hands, boosting me into the saddle; Andy pointing at stars—scatter. In between, other images rise to the surface. Andy reaching into a purse. Filling his hands with pill bottles. Hiding them in the Secret Pillow.

I don't recognize either Andy anymore.

I know what I want, though, regardless of Andy—and that's Sunny and Sam. Without Andy, winning that five hundred dollars is the *only* thing left that could turn Mom and Dad's maybe into a yes. I wanted to win before, but now I *need* to. The History Fair's on Thursday. I don't have much time to add anything new to my project.

But if I could catch one of the wild horses, bring it home, maybe even begin to train it—I could prove Jack's theory, and mine. What better way to demonstrate that history's important to the present than to show something from history that continued on, surviving even when nobody knew it? I couldn't *not* win.

And Andy would wish he had believed me.

In their stalls, Sunny and Sam stand tall, their ears pricked forward. I slip in next to Sam and lean against him, my forehead pressed into his side, my arms draped over his back. "You ready for an adventure?" I ask.

I take a little longer brushing him. I need to think this ride through, because it's dark now. Luckily there's a full moon, and I strap a head-lamp over my helmet for extra light. I have to stay focused: straight into the woods, then down the path where I always see the horses. I want to approach one, at least get her used to my voice and hands. I'll bring an extra halter and lead just in case.

My hands shake as I handle Sam's tack, and I have to take the whole saddle and blanket off, then put it on again, because I placed them too far back. Finally, slowly, I ease him out of the stable.

Cold snaps come so quick and sharp they make it hard to breathe. But they also happen every year, to remind us winter's coming, and I know how to deal with them by now. I already pulled on a neck warmer, plus my insulated barn coat and winter work gloves. Now I nestle my nose deeper into the neck warmer so I'm breathing into scratchy wool instead of knife-edged air.

But the woods are still just woods. Even with my headlight's beam casting a swath of bright light across the blue-black trees, I don't see the wild horses yet: no wisp of tail, no hoofprints.

"Come on," I murmur. "Show me where you are."

I look over my shoulder, and that's when I see her, all of her, standing right behind me. She's that beautiful foggy silver, with a black mane so long it drips past her neck line, and big round hooves. She blinks her liquid eyes in harsh light.

Then the other one comes up beside her, a little bigger, but with gentle eyes.

At first, Sam doesn't seem to notice. But when the horses start trotting, hooves punching through half-frozen leaves, he sidesteps, his mouth open and straining against the bit. Then he follows, in this awkward fast trot that's hard to sit. He's more excited than he was last time.

I can't let go of the reins. But somehow I need

to get closer, so I can catch one and prove what I know is true: that these horses are real. I need them to slow down.

But they don't. Sam trots even faster now, his head nodding. "Ho," I say, pulling a bit on the reins, sitting deep in the saddle. I want him to stay calm, but it isn't easy. The wild horses lead by moving beside Sam, like their presence alone can pull him in the right direction. When they veer away from the path we usually follow, the one that leads to the lake, I don't think much of it at first. But then I realize we're heading toward the mountain.

Suddenly my phone chimes. I take a quick glance in my pocket and struggle to read the words that bounce up and down in my hand.

It's Mom.

> You aren't out riding, are you?

My heart feels frozen. I know I'm breaking Mom's rule, but right now? I don't care.

> Dad and I need to know where you are. It's dark. I'll meet you at the barn.

The wild horses suddenly stop and plant their feet, nostrils flared. They've probably never heard the sound of a phone before. When horses go statue-still, it's hard to tell what they'll do next. They could bolt. Or rear. Or, rarely, just calm back down if they realize nothing's going to happen to them.

The phone beeps once more, but this time I don't look at it. Good thing I didn't try to take pictures. I just breathe.

The smaller wild horse leaps forward, her two front hooves stamping almost delicately into the ground. She starts running, and the other follows.

Sam does too. And then it's all I can do to hang on.

My ears fill with a rushing sound, not just the sparrows, and not just hooves. It's more than that. We whip past trees glowing in moonlight, moving too fast for me to get my bearings.

I didn't know the path went this far, but the wild horses are really running now, their necks stretched out.

Finally Sam skids to a stop in a small clearing,

and only then do I realize where the rushing sound is coming from. It seemed far away at first, but now it fills my ears. The wild horses aren't alone. From the edges of the woods, streams of shimmering silver and black begin to pour in, hooves pounding.

Ahead of us, there's an empty, curving path, scattered leaves, and trees clustered thick and dark.

But on either side, we're surrounded by horses.

CHAPTER 21

'm frozen. But not from cold. Clutching the reins, hoping Sam won't run again, I can't do anything but stare as rivers of horses course past, too many to count. I can't begin to think about catching one. There's no way to slow them down.

The phone won't matter now. I pull it out and snap one picture, two, three. But when I glance down, shining my headlamp, the pictures just look like gray blurs across my screen. I look back up, confused: Why don't even traces of their shapes come through?

Suddenly, the horses are gone.

It's hard to see any real hoofprints in the dirt. I swivel my head around, but I can't find a single sign of them—no quickly nodding heads, no swishing tails.

I sit awhile longer, Sam's breathing slow now. Then I see something.

If the moon hadn't glanced off the tree branch in that exact way, I probably would've missed it. But there it is: a strand of hair—so long and wiry-thick I know it came from one of the dappled horses' tails— stuck to the broken-off edge of a dead branch.

I stop Sam and softly slide off his back so I don't startle him. He's finally tired. So am I.

When I pluck the hair from the branch and hold it up to the light, it's a silvery black and even coarser than most horsehairs I've seen. It seems to shine, but in a way that makes it look like a beam of moonlight instead of a real hair that came off a real horse's tail. Then I remember my saddlebag, and I tuck the hair safely into it.

I keep Sam moving, trying to strike a balance between going quickly enough to get home fast and slowly enough to stay balanced. The ride is bumpier and slower than before, and I realize when I hear cracking under Sam's hooves that some tiny patches of ice have formed over the leaves, probably remnants from earlier rain and today's cold.

Just as I'm thinking I'll probably have to be extra careful now, Sam stumbles and I almost lose my seat. I have to grab the pommel of the saddle so I don't fall off.

"Hey, buddy," I say, hopping off and stroking his nose. "What happened to you?"

Check his legs, I think, my heart sinking. I know that's what Andy would do, right away. Sam's not the kind of horse to stumble. I run my hands down the back two, then the front, feeling for swelling. When I touch his right leg, he picks it up fast and kicks lightly back, away from my hand, not because he wants to hurt me, but just because he's trying to get away from some kind of pain.

My headlamp illuminates the scratch. It's a gash, really, not huge, but a little deeper and longer than an easy-to-heal cut.

No. I should have been paying closer attention.

I don't remember seeing anything sharp, but then again, when the horses were running, I didn't see much of anything. Who knows what Sam could've slashed, barreling up that path in the dark with all the others?

There's a small first-aid kit in my saddlebag, so I dab a little antiseptic on Sam's cut. Hopefully it will be enough to get him back to the barn. I pull the reins over his head and begin leading him slowly. Maybe I can sneak in and fix it up before Mom sees. Maybe it's small enough to heal overnight, though even as I think it, I know that's probably not true.

When we cross the pasture and I see the shadowy outline of Mom, standing in front of the barn with her hands on her hips, I know there's no way to hide. I lead Sam up to her and try to explain, but my words seem to fall apart in the cold air.

"Let me get this straight," Mom says. "*A*, you took Sam riding in the dark, on the coldest evening we've had yet this fall. *B*, you're always supposed to text me first. Obviously. And *C*, how did Sam cut himself? Remember the first rule—"

I break in before she can finish her sentence. "Always look out for the horses," I say. "I know. But Mom—I *was*. That's what I—"

She holds up her hand, cuts me off. "You know, I haven't forgotten your equine therapy idea. I've been reading more about it and thought it might actually work, as long as we could get Andy on board and convince your father. I planned to get started on some initial training exercises with Sam tomorrow when you were at school, to get a feel for how he might do. But with this cut, Sam won't be much use for a while."

"What?" Tears spring to my eyes, and my stomach wavers, sickness welling. Mom doesn't know about Andy's letter. She doesn't know Andy's not on board. I shut my eyes tight to squeeze that thought away, then open them again. If I win the prize, Andy might not need to be on board, at least not right away. "It's only a little cut, though, right?"

"It's deep enough to worry about," Mom says. "I'll have to keep an eye on it, make sure it doesn't get infected." She looks at me and her eyes smolder like coals. "You don't want Sam going lame, do you?"

I shake my head, my throat thick. Sparrows flutter out of their nests and whirl around my shoulders.

"You'll help me, then," Mom says. "We'll have to tend to the wound every day."

"Yes," I whisper. Tears cloud my eyes and I rest a hand on Sam's warm neck. I was thinking too much about the wild horses, and not about the one right in front of me. I open my mouth to apologize, but Mom holds up a hand and shakes her head.

"I'm too upset to talk more right now," she says. "Clean and bandage the cut properly. I'll come back to check on him later." Then she stalks off, her arms crossed.

I lead Sam into the barn, put him in cross-ties. After I've cleaned his cut as gently as I can with water and saline solution, I apply ointment and wrap a padded bandage around his leg. He stands still, his head hanging just a little.

"I'm sorry, buddy," I whisper. Then I lead him

into his stall and make sure he has hay and fresh water.

My phone sits like a stone in my pocket. My fingers go to it, then draw back. I remember Maya's face, the soft chill of her voice when she said, *Then maybe you'll understand.* I've made so many mistakes today, but I know at least one I can try to fix. Maybe two.

I breathe into and through the wings that fill my chest. *What if Maya doesn't want to talk to me? Not just now, but ever?*

But then I remember Nari's reading: *Isn't it easy to want to control everything that happens?* And Sharon's word: *honesty.*

I thought I knew what Andy would say about equine therapy, but I didn't. I can't know how Maya's going to feel either.

But that doesn't mean I can't try to make things better.

I start and delete about ten texts before I settle on the simplest one:

> Hey can we talk?

Even before the dots appear that show she's writing back, I can already feel the healing start, a bandage patching up the torn parts of my heart.

Not because I know how things are going to turn out, but because I did what I needed to do.

Ping. I look down and see just one word:

Sure.

The next day during lunch we eat fast, not saying much. But it feels good to sit together.

Maya takes a swig of chocolate milk. "Ready?"

I pop one last grape in my mouth. "Let's go."

Since our school is small, with nine grades in one building, we still have a playground, plus the basketball court and soccer field. We eat lunch at a different time than the little kids, and it's kind of funny how many of us decide to use the slide and merry-go-round once we're done.

Maya and I sit side by side on two of the swings. It's been ages since I actually pumped as hard as I could and soared into the sky. But it feels good to rock my legs back and forth while I think about what to say.

I fumble around with some explanations and unfinished sentences, but as soon as I say "I'm sorry," Maya's face relaxes, and I continue. "I thought about it and…I know it's not your fault that your dad told Andy to go to rehab. It's not your dad's fault either. Jail would have made sense too. Lots of people have to do that."

"Like I said, he was only trying to help Andy." Maya twists her swing a little ways toward me, then lets it fall back again. "In the long run, I mean. He had to think about the law too."

"I get that," I say. "I've been trying to figure out what to think about Andy, honestly. At first, I didn't think that what he did was actually *him*."

"It's kind of funny that you can believe in wild horses you barely see, but not in something that for sure happened," Maya says quietly. It might sound mean, but I know it's not. It's just true. And I haven't forgotten what Sharon said about honesty.

"Well, I guess it's more about what I *want* to

believe," I say. "And now Andy's the one I'm mad at. I can't figure him out."

"Well, my dad said that what makes the whole thing really hard is that the people he has to sentence are often great people who just happen to have this problem." She's looking at me, and her eyes are kind. "Maybe Andy isn't one thing or the other, you know? Maybe he's both."

For a while, I can't speak. The words clump together in my throat. I feel like Mr. Hamilton, wondering how his dad could have been completely wrong when someone in the same room is trying to prove that he might have been right.

All I end up saying is "I hope so." Then Maya pushes her swing near mine and hugs my shoulder.

"How's your dad?" I ask.

"Much better," Maya says. "He's on a special medicine, and they're giving him all these anti-stress techniques too."

"That's awesome." Relief washes through me. I really want Mr. Gonzalez to be okay.

"It's a start," Maya says.

"So…are we good?" I look at her, trying to read her eyes.

She smiles. "We're good."

Other students start to stream out the cafeteria doors. Some roll themselves down the huge hill at the end of the playground. Others head toward the field: we aren't allowed to have leaf fights, but apparently football is okay, even though those games usually get intense.

Jamila and Cory sit in the two empty swings next to Maya and me.

"Hey, guys," Jamila says. "You nervous about the History Fair?"

"Not really." But Maya's words don't match her voice. She's put more effort into her project than pretty much anyone else.

"I think I'm prepared," Cory says.

"Ha." Jamila rolls her eyes. "If by 'prepared' you mean you spend all your time editing this one single video you're using instead of making sure you have all the required sources, then—yes! You're prepared!"

"She's harsh." Cory looks at us pleadingly, but Maya just laughs.

"Be more like her," Jamila says, nodding toward Maya, "with her binders and notes all organized. Then I'll stop giving you a hard time."

"How about you, Claire?" Cory asks. "Are you ready?"

I think about my poster, divided into its neat sections. All I'm missing is a horse.

"As ready as possible." My voice sounds pretty confident, even to me.

"Well," Cory says, hopping off the swing, "since nobody's defending me, I'm going to have to throw some leaves at *all* of you."

Jamila grabs a handful and lobs it at his jacket. "Beat you to it."

"Hey!" Cory says, hurling some back. "At least it's supposed to snow tomorrow. I'll get revenge with some serious snowballs."

Then Maya tosses a bunch of leaves at me. "That's for getting mad at me," she says, but she's smiling.

Pretty soon we're all laughing and throwing leaves. We manage to squeeze in about two minutes' worth before Mr. Jenkins notices and yells at us to stop.

CHAPTER 22

would rather ride Sam. There's no question about that. Especially since the snow Cory talked about has started, tiny flakes drifting from a gray sky.

But a lot has happened since the pheasant spooked Sunny and the world sped by so fast I thought it was going to turn upside down. I think she and I will be okay.

We need to be. I still need to catch one of the horses and make sure the tunnel I saw at Pine Lake leads where I think it does.

The question is how to ride Sunny without

Mom noticing. After what happened to Sam, she won't want me taking horses anywhere.

But Sunny doesn't know that. And when I put on first her saddle blanket, smoothing the hair underneath it, then the saddle, cinching it tight, she doesn't budge. She swings her neck around to look at me once, her eyes big, kind, searching my face. Trusting me. Next comes the bridle, the cold bit and the throatlatch, then leading her around the back of the barn so Mom doesn't see.

Now I'm on Sunny and she's picking her hooves up high, her haunches coiled up under her, ears pricked forward. I'm trying to sit heavy, knowing she'll be able to sense it the moment I hesitate. It's hard, because the truth is, I'm nervous.

We follow the edge of a cornfield, sandwiched between forest and fields. Snow falls lightly, like lace. We have to be careful of the fence line—I don't want her getting tangled up in anything, and sometimes when a piece of fence is down it's hard to see clearly. Wire can cut into a horse's skin fast and leave pencil-thin gashes up and down their legs, worse than Sam's.

Plus, horses panic when they get caught, and panic makes everything worse. I know that from experience. When my flutter feeling starts, nothing seems to work out right.

Even though Sunny moves quickly, it takes a long time to get to the part of Cedar Lake I'm trying to reach. I try not to think too hard about the snow, and I do arm circles to keep my upper body warm.

There's a mountain-biking trail that circles all of Cedar Lake, but it's much too narrow and rocky for me to attempt riding Sunny around it. Fortunately, there's also an area before the beginning of the trail that's set up with a few benches and a bike rack. I figure I can leave Sunny there. She'll be safe long enough for me to at least figure out if my guesses about this tunnel are correct.

As I slide off Sunny's back and tie her to a tree near the bike rack, I grab the stone from the box and close my eyes. *Tell me where to go*, I think.

It would be weird to say the stone pulls me. After all, I'm holding it in my hand. But the air's shimmering again, and I feel like I'm going where I need to. Like a magnet's drawing me through the trees while cedar leaves brush against my skin. And sure enough, a cavern opens up, right where the lake meets the forest floor.

It's exactly what I expected. Ringing the hollow are piles of beautiful black stones, just like the one from my box. Just like the ones from Pine Lake. The land curves, and I'll have to step a bit into the water to see the opening up close.

I sink my foot about a half an inch deep. My boots are thick, and they don't leak. Carefully, I move about two feet toward the hollow, holding the stone.

It looks just like the cavern on Pine Lake. Taller than I am, lined with sand and stone, and wide enough for a horse to pick her way through.

I close my eyes and I can practically see them: the wild horses. I can see their story unfolding right in front of me.

They tumbled into the hole in the ice here at Cedar Lake. At first the cold water shocked them, made them sputter. Jack, his wet arm stuck to the ice, pulling himself up and up, would have watched them sink, his eyes blurring with tears. The cold would have set into his limbs as he forced himself to turn away and worked to climb back onto the still-frozen ice.

But the horses somehow swam together, the wagon snapping loose behind them. And far below the surface of the water, where everyone thought they'd find their bones one day, the horses found a path out instead. A tunnel, dry and safe. They walked through and through, until they ended up at Pine Lake, where the shore was easy to reach and the woods thick and the mountains high. They climbed free of the tunnel and shed the last of their harnesses over frozen ice, and when spring came the tack floated into the lapping water for Jack to find a piece of it.

I scoop a few handfuls of stones into my saddle-bag. They'll be perfect to display for my project, alongside the horseshoe Mr. Hamilton found.

Then I scramble back up the bank, through the trees, shouldering the saddlebag that got a whole lot heavier. "Oh, Sunny! Guess what I've got for us!" I push through to the path and the bike rack and—

Sunny isn't tied up anymore. She's gone.

She was *just* here.

It hasn't been that long since I made my way down to the lake. Has it? I check my phone.

Ten minutes—okay, longer than I thought. But still, she's waited that long before. Did she get spooked, without Sam by her side? Did someone take her? Hardly anybody comes down these paths when it's snowing. I look wildly around, cold air catching in my throat, a mix of leaves and snow crunching under my boots as I spin. Inside my chest, wings flutter awake.

"Sunny!" I call again, loudly singing her name. My voice echoes off the mountain on the other side of the lake. "Sun-*ny!*"

The snow's falling more heavily and I suddenly remember walking through the woods with Andy in winter, how when I was littler he'd help me figure out which animals had passed through the forest because of their tracks. "Snow tells stories," he'd say, then he'd kneel down and point to deep impressions, fresh powder just kicked out the back or compacted in wet ice. *Deer. Fox. Possum.* And once—*Bear.*

Snow. Fresh snow will tell me where to go. I need to look down, not up. And when I do, I find the first hoofprint. Then the second. I follow them, hoping they'll wind up the path and cut into the woods past the lake, the ones that eventually run into cornfields and down to my house.

Gray and green branches brush my sleeves. The first blue jays of winter dive in front of my eyes. I walk and walk. As long as I follow Sunny's hoofprints faster than they fill in with new snow, I should find her eventually.

There's one major problem with my plan. I don't know where I am.

I mean, I know the general direction of home. But it isn't hard to get turned around in the woods. The snow makes it easy to see where I've been, but it's tricky to tell how far I need to go…and it's cold.

I check my phone: no reception. That's typical by this lake because the mountains are wedged so close together, they cut the signal. The sparrows skitter against my bones, brushing their soft feathers along my heart. I shiver.

It's okay, I think. *You'll find her.*

The woods are shadowy now, not quite dark but getting there. Fading light on the blue-white snow is all I have. The hoofprints go on and on.

I keep walking, the stones knocking together in my saddlebag. My legs move steadily, but they burn. I need a rest, just for a minute. I lean against a tree and close my eyes while branches crack and sigh above my head.

Then, like thunder, a pounding. But not from the sky. It's from somewhere else, farther up the mountain. My eyes fly open. I look around.

Hooves, curling up, then striking the ground. Tails, streaked with silver. Outstretched necks. I rub my eyes, trying to adjust to the growing dark.

The hooves slow a little as they bear down beside me, then widen and turn until I realize I'm surrounded by a circle of horses. They look at me with their liquid eyes, calm as ponds. They nicker softly, air whooshing through their soft noses. They bow their heads.

"I don't know where to go," I say out loud.

One of the horses tosses her head and I follow

the motion, up to the top of what I now see is my favorite maple tree, the one with low branches and a huge V right in the middle, close enough that even when I was little I could always climb up, nestle in, and see far.

I thought I was so far away. But I'm almost home.

I follow the path to where the forest empties out in the pasture by our barn. A light, cold breeze brushes over my cheeks.

For just one moment, I turn back toward the trees.

A swish of tail, midnight black and the color of the moon.

Dappled-gray legs, dancing away.

Come back, I think. *I need to catch you.*

But that thought wisps away as another one grows. *Sunny.* I need to find Sunny.

"Claire?" a voice calls from inside the barn. A voice I know, but haven't heard in so long it feels like a dream. "Is that you?"

My throat feels locked and dry. I stoop to grab a handful of snow and stuff it in my mouth, hoping it will get my tongue back to normal. "Um, yeah?" I call. I rise, open the barn door, and tiptoe in, past the hay wagon, to the stable.

Sunny's there. In her stall next to Sam, crunching grain.

And the voice belongs to exactly who I thought it did.

Andy.

"How are you here?" I whisper.

"How are *you* here?" he shoots back. "Mom and Dad are freaking out! Dad's in the woods looking for you, and Mom's at the house hoping you'll show up. When we saw Sunny here with her tack on, we had no idea where you could be. She told me to wait here just in case."

I cross my arms over my chest. I have no idea how Sunny ended up back in her stall, but I decide to pretend like I'm not confused. Besides, I can't believe Andy's acting like it's no big deal for him to just show up. "I was in the woods. Seriously, how did you get here?"

"I was going to surprise you," he says. "I told Mom and Dad not to say anything, and I guess they didn't. I really want to get started with my agricultural mechanics program."

I can't believe he's finally home. Part of me wants to reach out, take his hand. But my arms feel stuck in place.

"So you just decided to leave? They didn't make you stay?" Even as I speak them, the words sound soft and full of wonder. I sit on a hay bale and rub my shoulder, which hurts a lot, maybe from how I was lying down.

"They can't," Andy says. "I completed my full required time, so after that Starshine Center is voluntary. I thought I might stay longer, but my therapists did say I was making such great progress that it would be okay to leave. They're setting me up with some meetings to go to here so I can stay on track."

My head spins; the sparrows whirl. Then I feel something inside me harden. My voice turns cold. "Required *time*? If you could have left earlier, then why did you stay longer?"

Andy takes both my hands in his. "I knew it was the right thing, Little C. There's a lot that I need to explain to you, stuff that was just too hard to say in a letter."

I'm sure Andy wants to tell me the truth, even though I already know it. My heart somersaults. Seeing his face, his crooked baseball cap, his eyes with the stars in them, makes the cold in my voice crack open. "I missed you. I really wanted you to be here."

"I know." Andy squeezes my hands, then lets them go. "But it was good for me."

"What about the rest of us, though?" Now my voice sounds as hard as the strike of a hoof on pavement. "What if it wasn't good for *us*?" Andy's extra time at Starshine meant more money. More loneliness and worry.

Andy bows his head and pushes his baseball cap back.

I grab my saddlebag and unzip it a little too roughly. "Look," I say. "I know you don't believe me about the horses, but I have proof. I—"

But the hair has disappeared. I dig through the stones, down to the bottom of the bag, but it's gone.

"Never mind." My voice feels like it's going to burst into flame. I shake the saddlebag and fistfuls of stones tumble like water to the barn floor, black and silver, smooth and cold, more than I realized I'd taken.

Andy smiles, but his eyes are sad. "Hey, cool. Worry stones. You remembered." He picks one up and rubs it in his palm. "Thanks, Little C."

"I'm the one who really needs those," I snap. "All I've been doing is *worrying* about you. And about the horses—like how I'll ever figure out how to keep them, without you to help! Meanwhile, you were just trying to figure out what you could do without *us*!" The flame inside reaches so high it fills my eyes, and tears gather and spill.

Andy reaches out and touches my elbow, but I flinch. I need to finish my project before tomorrow, and being around Andy makes it hard to focus.

I leave him there in the barn with my saddle-bag, surrounded by stones.

CHAPTER 23

I'm running, breath heaving, feet pounding the path leading from the barn to the house. I have no idea what I'll say to Mom when I arrive. I just need to get away from Andy.

At the porch, I stop short, double over with my hands on my knees. Slowly, I open the door.

Mom rushes out from the living room. "Claire!" she says, squeezing my shoulders, her knuckles white. "Where did you go? We were worried sick."

"Why is he here?" I ask.

Mom's face falls. She can see I'm not smiling.

"I know it's a surprise. But honestly, Claire, it was a surprise for us too. He just called us last night."

"It wouldn't have been that difficult to tell me." My voice is hard as stone.

Mom sighs. "We were planning to talk to you tonight, then pick Andy up as a family tomorrow, but then Starshine said it would be best to do the pickup today, and we couldn't find you. Haven't you gotten my texts?"

"I didn't check." After school, I'd stuck my head in the door and yelled "Barn!" without waiting for Mom's or Dad's answer. Turns out they were gone.

"But that was one of the rules, Claire." Mom's voice is tired. "We weren't too worried at first, but by the time we realized you weren't at Maya's or the barn and the snow had started, I was really scared. We all were."

"Where's Dad?" I ask.

"He's been out in the woods, looking for you," Mom says. "Andy texted us both when you got to the barn. He should be back soon."

"So Andy's just—here now?" When he left, our house felt so strange, so empty and quiet. But now the strangeness comes from knowing he's here, filling all the rooms back up with something I don't know if I want. "Does he know about the pills I found?"

"We went to the pharmacy together and got rid of them," Mom says. "All three of us. First thing."

Just then, the porch door opens and Dad and Andy come in, stomping their feet.

"Claire!" Dad rushes to me. Then he holds me at arm's length, looks hard into my face. "I don't know whether to hug you or scream at you. Where have you *been*?"

"In the woods," I whisper. The thickening trees, the darkness falling, the whirling snow and pounding hooves—it feels like a dream.

Dad shakes his head. "Well, we're going to have to revisit this whole riding arrangement, especially now that winter's coming." He glances at Mom.

"It doesn't matter. I don't have that much more time left with them anyway." I can hear the dullness in my voice. Without one of the wild horses, I'll just have a normal project; my chances of winning the money will be slimmer. I don't know how the equine therapy plan can work.

Dad sighs, looks at the floor.

"Who's hungry?" Andy asks.

Nobody says anything.

"You know what sounds good?" Andy says. "Pizza."

Silence swells, so thick it feels like a bubble closing all of us in.

"Come on," Andy pleads. "I haven't had it in forever. Starshine had good food, but it wasn't takeout pizza, you know?"

"Okay," Mom finally says. "Pizza does sound good."

"I'll go pick it up." Andy grabs his keys from the counter.

Mom and Dad look nervously at each other. "I can get it!" Mom says brightly.

"I can too," Dad says.

"Um. So can I." Andy starts to head out the door, but then Dad grabs the keys.

"Hang on, son," he says. "Why don't you let one of us come with you?"

"Hey!" Andy reaches for the keys, but Dad quickly sticks them in his pocket. Then Andy lets go of the doorknob and crosses his arms over his chest. "Okay. I know what's going on here."

"There's nothing going on," Mom says, her smile too big. "We just think it would be good for you to—you know. Have some company."

"Because you don't trust me." Andy sounds worn out, but there's an edge in his voice too.

The bubble of silence swells again, shimmering. We're all stuck in it. Words jumble inside me, mixed with flutters and stabs of heat.

Dad clears his throat. "Well," he says. "Trust is something you have to build. Especially when you've already knocked it down a few times."

Andy shakes his head. "Unbelievable," he says. "See, this is why I knew I wouldn't be able to live here. You'll never really believe I changed."

"Well, have you?" I blurt out. "How do we know you won't steal from Mom and Dad again?"

Andy looks at me, his eyes so sad I almost wish I hadn't said the words. Still, I had to let them out.

When he answers me, he's not angry, just quiet. "I don't know how to prove it, Little C. I just know I'm different now. Starshine really helped."

"It will take time," Mom says softly. "For all of us. But for now, how about you go get the pizza?" She motions toward the door. "Pepperoni, please. Lots of it."

Dad opens his mouth to speak, but then he closes it. Hands the keys to Andy.

Andy looks from Mom to Dad, and then to me. "Thanks, guys," he says. "I'll be back soon."

The pizza's perfectly hot, the cheese still bubbling.

We chew in silence. From the outside, I know it looks like any of the family dinners we used to have, back before Starshine and all the rest. But from the inside, it feels completely different.

It feels like when I have Sam all tacked up and I bring him outside and realize he's been puffing his chest out to make the cinch way looser than it needs to be. I have to tighten it again and again to make sure the saddle will stay put when I step into the stirrup.

When Andy came back from the restaurant in record time holding a just-made pizza, our family's cinch tightened just a little. But it'll still be a while before I feel like the saddle's on quite right.

"Have you guys been going to those support group meetings?" Andy asks.

"I have," I say.

"It sounded like you're starting to like them." Andy smiles.

"The other kids are really cool." I think about how it will feel to talk in the next meeting and tell everyone about Andy coming back, how I'll always have a place to bring my words now.

Andy turns to Mom and Dad. "Do you guys go?"

Mom flushes. "I meant to."

Dad looks down at his plate and shakes his head. "I can see how maybe we should give it a try."

"I guess I thought Starshine was doing everything for you that could be done," Mom says.

"Yeah, but the meetings aren't really for Andy," I say. "They're for me."

Mom looks confused. "What do you mean by that, Claire?"

"Andy has this problem," I say. "But even

though I love him, I can't fix it. I have to think about myself too. The meetings help me do that."

Andy smiles. "Bingo," he says quietly.

There's a knock at the door. "Huh," Mom says. "Wonder who that is." She scoots her chair back and heads out to the porch. "Nate!" she says. "What a surprise."

Andy coughs in the middle of a bite of pizza, has to work hard to chew and swallow it. His face goes totally pale.

"I got it, Mom," he says, rushing to the door.

"Nate hasn't come around in ages!" Mom gushes. "We need to chat."

Dad starts to get up, but Andy beats him to the door and steps just in front of Mom. "No, seriously," he says. "I've got this."

I freeze, clench my hands at my sides. When Mom opened the door, a flock of sparrows rushed in and caught my heart.

"It's cool that you're home," Nate says, slapping Andy on the back. "You should come out with us tonight."

Andy shakes his head. "No, thanks."

"Oh, come on." Nate punches his arm. "Everyone wants to see you."

"I'm going to stick around here," Andy says.

"Whatever, dude." Nate peeks into the kitchen, catches my eyes, and looks away. "Hey, can I go up to your room, though? Grab that textbook I left?"

Hearing Nate and Andy, I feel the flutter inside me grow. I look at Mom and Dad, and they're listening too. Dad's eyes narrow and he starts to stand up again, then sits when Andy's voice comes through strong.

"No way, man. I told you in the text," Andy says. "I'm done with that."

"I didn't think you were actually serious." Nate takes a step back, then drops his voice so low I barely hear it. "Where are they, though?"

"Gone." Andy's voice is cold.

"Wow." Nate shakes his head. His face flushes red, but his eyes look hard, sharp. "Well, I'm heading out. Good luck, bud. Let me know if you change your mind."

He leaves, and Andy turns back around, softly shuts the door. His shoulders stoop forward; he rubs the back of his neck. When he returns to the kitchen, he looks older somehow.

"What was that about?" Mom asks.

Andy shakes his head. "Nothing," he says. "I just don't think we'll be hanging out much anymore."

Dad looks carefully at Andy. He leans back, rests his chin in one hand. "Maybe for the best, huh?"

"Definitely." Andy nods, looks at me.

The cinch tightens one more notch.

CHAPTER 24

I wake up in darkness, too early, sparrows swooping through my chest. My insides are empty and crowded at the same time, and all I want to do is crawl out of my skin. I've never woken up with this feeling before, but as soon as I open my eyes, I remember Sam's cut, Andy coming back, Sunny running away, the wild horses bringing me home. Memories gather inside like a storm and sweep over every part of me.

When I get downstairs, I find Mom and Dad in the kitchen already, drinking coffee. Mom takes one look at me and comes over, puts her arm around my shoulders. "Claire?" she asks. "Are you okay? You're trembling."

I take a deep breath, but even that's shaky. I feel like my whole body has turned into one big wing that could fly away.

At first I can't answer Mom. I just shake my head. Dad comes to stand on my other side, and with both of them holding on to me, I feel some of the shakiness pass.

"I'm just really, really…worried," I finally say. It's the only word I can put on the feeling, even if it seems like more than that. "It makes me feel fluttery inside."

Dad gently guides me toward my usual chair.

"You've been feeling that way more lately, haven't you?" Mom asks. "I could tell that day in the car, when I picked you up at Maya's."

"Yeah." I didn't think she had noticed. "Deep breathing helps. And also, just waiting. Being by myself until it goes away."

"Hon," Dad says, "feeling worried is part of life. But sometimes when it gets to affect your body like that, it might mean you're dealing with something called anxiety. I see it in my students a lot."

"Do you think some of this might have to do with Andy being back?" Mom asks softly. "I know you weren't expecting it."

"Maybe." Last night with Andy, I left the dinner table early, saying I needed to work on my project—which was true. It just wasn't the *whole* truth. The whole truth had a lot to do with not knowing how to feel about Andy.

"The point," Dad continues, "is that a little bit of anxiety is normal, but a lot can be a reason to get some extra help. Talking to someone can be a good start."

"Let's keep an eye on it, okay?" Mom says. "It's good that you figured out the deep breathing. But keep communicating with us. If it feels like it's getting to be too much, like it's happening too often, we can look at next steps." She reaches out and hugs me twice. "One for love, one for good luck," she whispers.

"Okay," I say. That seems fair. Feeling Mom's and Dad's hands on me and listening to the air go in and out of my mouth as I breathe and talk, I can tell it's getting a little better. For now.

In the afternoon, Maya and I set up our presentations right next to each other.

"Are you nervous?" she asks. She knows I am—she's just trying to keep me talking. "Want to do another quick run-through with me?"

"No, thanks." I've practiced enough in front of my bedroom mirror, so I think going over it again would make me more nervous.

I turn around to look at my poster, and Maya stands beside me. "It looks really great," she says.

"Thanks." I can't help smiling. My poster has pictures of Jack Hamilton, a blown-up copy of the article, a topographical map showing Cedar Lake and Pine Lake, pictures of logging, sugaring, and farming equipment, and a list of the steps to take to establish an equine therapy business along with some examples of successful businesses in other places. On the table where my poster is propped up, I've placed the box with each of its contents labeled, plus a small pile of extra stones, the horse-shoe, and a description I added:

THE LEGEND OF THE LAKES

Almost a hundred years ago, Jack Hamilton survived a dangerous fall through the ice on Cedar Lake. Although everyone was grateful he made it out alive, he and his family mourned their team of horses, which fell through the ice and were never found. They had been used in all the important ways horses were back then: for farming tasks and transportation. Losing them was a big deal.

But Jack was convinced they hadn't been lost at all. He believed his horses had survived. After finding pieces of their harness floating in a different body of water, Pine Lake, he knew they must have escaped somehow. Could a secret underground tunnel connect Pine Lake with Cedar Lake? Did the horses find it, and travel through the underwater tunnel until they came out the other side? Whatever Jack believed, he hung on to it for the rest of his life. Even today, if you're looking closely, you can find evidence of wild horses in the woods surrounding Pebble Mountain. Maybe they're descendants of those fallen horses. Maybe Jack was right.

I don't have the horse I wanted to catch. Still, my project combines everything I've learned and believe, and it does what Ms. Larkin said it should do: It shows the past and the future, including *my* future. How it's all connected.

But Maya's project looks even more amazing. She decided to do a Google Slides presentation, and it includes a video she made, reenacting one of Edna Beard's speeches on the House floor. She also has all kinds of information about how Edna Beard influenced law today, and how she personally would implement Edna's values in her own career. Maya even dressed up for this, in a long-sleeved black dress with a fancy collar pinned to it. She's speaking *as* Edna Beard too, so everyone who comes to look at her presentation can feel like they're interviewing Edna Beard herself.

Everyone else from our class is spread across the great room in the community center, and Ms. Larkin lets us all take a few minutes to walk around and look at one another's work.

It's pretty cool to see what my classmates have done. Cory's project shows the history of film, with pictures of old movie scenes and explanations of how techniques in film have evolved over time. He even has two versions of *Aladdin* playing to demonstrate how the same story can be portrayed differently. For her fashion project, Jamila sketched dozens of outfits from different decades. Around the room, there are presentations on cars, cooking, historical figures, and sports.

Ms. Larkin goes to the front of the room and clears her throat. "Okay, students! It's about time to let that hard work shine."

I feel my hands shake a little. It's the sparrows, skittering against my wrists. *Shhhh*, I tell them.

"The judges will be coming in soon. Remember, they'll walk around the room looking at projects, and they'll stop in small groups and expect you to explain the work you've done. Be ready to answer questions too!" Ms. Larkin gives us two thumbs-up. "I know you'll all do great."

But I don't know for sure. My face feels hot and splotchy.

When Ms. Larkin opens the door and the first judges walk in, Maya nudges me. "Don't twist your hands so much," she says. "Keep them behind your back."

She's right. I was squeezing my fingers together so hard my knuckles turned white.

There are about twenty judges altogether, and they spread themselves out across the room. I see three people making their way to my poster. I know one of them: Mr. Bailey, who's the head of the library. I haven't seen the other two before. But then a fourth person comes through the community center door and looks right at me. As soon as I see him, I feel a smile stretching across my face. It's Mr. Hamilton.

"Hello, Claire," Mr. Bailey says. "Nice to see you here, and what an interesting project!" He squints at the title: "Horses at Work."

"Um, thanks." My voice is squeaking. I clear

my throat and start over. "Thanks for coming to take a look." I breathe in through my nose, out through my mouth.

"I'm Ms. Wallace," another judge says, sticking her hand out. That's when I realize I should probably shake everyone's hand. I blush, wishing I'd thought of that on my own.

"Nice to meet you," I say. Then I shake Mr. Bailey's hand too, and the other judge's, a woman named Ms. DeSoto. It's hard for me to look right in their eyes, but Ms. Larkin said eye contact was important, so I force myself to glance at each of them for a moment.

Then it's time to greet Mr. Hamilton. "Thank you so much for coming," I say.

"Wouldn't miss it." Mr. Hamilton winks.

Then we all just stand there, smiling at one another.

"Oh," I say, realizing I'm supposed to start. "Sorry."

Ms. DeSoto shakes her head. "No need to apologize, Claire," she says. "When you're ready, we'd love to hear about your project."

For a second, I forget everything I'd planned to say. I can't even remember my first sentence. I close my eyes for just a second so I don't have to see all their serious, curious faces staring at me, waiting for me to talk.

That split-second with my eyes closed is all I need. I remember. And when I open my eyes, I'm ready.

For the awards ceremony, we're all supposed to sit with our families in the audience. It's not hard to find Mom, Dad, and Andy, who wave at me frantically as soon as Ms. Larkin taps the mic and tells everyone to start moving toward the audience area. I sit at the end of the row, next to Dad, even though there's a spare seat by Andy too. I'm just not quite ready to talk to him.

"It's such a pleasure to be here for another History Fair!" Ms. Larkin says. "Thanks to our community judges, who work hard to assess each presentation fairly. And thanks, of course, to these amazing students who surprise me every year with how innovative they can be. I think this might be our best year yet."

She probably says that every year, but I still smile. We *did* all do a pretty good job.

Even so, the flutter feeling is coming back, not as strong as it did when I woke up this morning, but definitely noticeable. I breathe deeply and try to tell myself: *What's the worst that could happen? Sometimes it isn't as bad as we think it will be.*

But the worst that could happen is that I don't win. I don't get the money. And that wouldn't be so bad if it didn't mean also not being able to pay for the Therapeutic Riding Instructor certification, which would put us even further away from the therapy business.

And then we'll definitely have to sell Sunny and Sam.

So actually, the worst is pretty bad.

I clench my fists together, trying to focus on Ms. Larkin's words instead of the birds tumbling inside.

"I'm so excited to announce the winner of this

year's prize," she says. "This person's project exhibited extensive knowledge, creativity, and an ability to appreciate how the past influences the present."

That could be my project, I think. *But it could also be—*

"Maya Gonzalez," Ms. Larkin says. "Could you please come to the front of the room?"

My fingernails dig into my palms and I look for Maya a couple of rows ahead. She takes a quick look back at me, her eyes wide and full of something I can't pinpoint: It's not quite sadness, but it looks a little like that.

That's it, I think. *That was my chance, and I lost it.*

I watch Maya accept the certificate Ms. Larkin gives her and shake hands again with the judges. When we all get up to leave, I give Maya a big hug. Her project was perfect, and she doesn't deserve to feel worried or upset about me not winning.

"Congratulations," I say, trying not to cry.

"Thanks, Claire. We're so proud of Maya," Mr. Gonzalez says, his hand on her shoulder. He seems much better already. And seeing the way Maya looks up at him, her eyes shining, makes me feel like the award went to the right person.

Still, cold disappointment settles in my stomach. I picture Sunny and Sam in their stalls, and tears gather in the corners of my eyes.

Mom grabs my hand and squeezes. "Your project looked great, Claire," she says. "You really did your best."

Andy has his hands stuffed in his pockets, but he smiles at me. I can tell he wants to give me a hug but isn't sure if I want one. And I'm not sure I do either.

"Pretty awesome presentation, Little C.," he says. "What did they think about your legend?"

"I don't think they believed it," I say. "But they thought it was interesting."

"I didn't really see that coming," Dad says. "But no wonder you've been wanting to go into the woods more often."

"I'll have to take you there. You'll see." As we head toward the door, I notice Mr. Hamilton standing off to the side. He seems to be waiting for us.

"Hello, Barton family," he says. "It's good to

see you all again." Then he focuses on Andy. "And it's nice to officially meet you, young man."

"You too, sir." Andy shakes his hand.

"Claire, your take on my father's story was certainly interesting," Mr. Hamilton says. "I love 'The Legend of the Lakes.'"

"Thanks," I say. "I wish I could have met Jack. I think he would've liked my theory."

"I'm sure he would have," Mr. Hamilton says. "But it's your equine therapy plan that really struck me. I think it would be quite beneficial for our community."

"It certainly would," Dad says. "It's too bad that we—"

"I have a proposal for you," Mr. Hamilton says, holding up his hand. "When I sold my horses, I wasn't really thinking clearly. I was sad about my grandkids being far away and thought it was time to move on to something else. But meeting Claire changed that."

Mom, Dad, and Andy all look at me, their expressions a mix of smiles and raised eyebrows.

"Claire reminded me of the good that horses

can do," Mr. Hamilton continues. "And, maybe more important, of how much we all need to keep going, no matter how hard it seems." He takes a deep breath. "Now we have a problem. Claire has this great idea for an equine therapy business, and she also has horses, but facilities and money are issues. Meanwhile, I've got this terrific barn and indoor arena, but—" He pauses and looks at me with a smile in his eyes.

"No horses?" I ask.

"You got it. No horses," he says.

Puzzle pieces start clicking together in my mind, but I can't let myself really believe what Mr. Hamilton's suggesting until he says it out loud.

"What about starting your equine therapy business at my barn?" Mr. Hamilton asks.

Mom's jaw drops. "Wow," she says. "It's incredibly generous of you to offer. But"—she looks at Dad, then at me, her forehead wrinkling again—"affording the horses has become quite difficult. Financially, it's too hard for us right now."

"I understand," Mr. Hamilton says. "But what I mean is, you could move Sunny and Sam to my barn. I'd be happy to keep them as my own and assume the costs. Honestly, taking care of horses again would be good for me. And Claire could come over to ride anytime. Well, you'd all be there, as needed for the business."

The floor seems to cave in beneath me. Sunny and Sam—gone, yet still with me.

It's a path I didn't see, didn't ask for.

But maybe it could work.

"I could help train too," Mr. Hamilton adds. "I don't think I've gotten too rusty."

Mom's eyes widen and Dad says: "Are you sure?"

But Mr. Hamilton's already nodding. "Yes, yes," he says. "It would be a good start. Then we'll see where it goes. I'd like to think about adding more horses, actually. If the business expands, you'll want more than one or two anyway."

I feel the wings again, fluttering free, but this time they're lifting me so high in the air I think I could touch the clouds.

CHAPTER 25

I'm in the barn, measuring grain, when Andy walks in. Mom and Dad say he'll be staying at the house for another week, just long enough to find his own apartment and get enrolled in his agricultural mechanics program. That's about as much time I have before we load Sunny and Sam into the trailer and bring them to their new home with Mr. Hamilton. I've already texted Nari, and she and Pia are going to be our first customers. They're coming to his place as soon as Pia's back, which might not be for a while. But that's okay, because we have our certification to complete, plus we need to set up Mr. Hamilton's barn and riding ring. And Sam needs to heal. Fortunately, Mom says his cut is looking better already.

I thought I'd feel sadder, having Andy and my horses close by, yet not really here.

But actually, I feel okay.

"Hey," Andy says. "How do leaves get from place to place?"

I roll my eyes. "Oh my gosh, are you serious?"

"Very." Andy nods solemnly. "You have ten seconds to answer. Ten, nine…"

"Okay, fine." I can't help smiling. This is one of Andy's oldest jokes. "With an *autumn*obile."

"Excellent work," he says. "The amazing pre-senter is also an amazing joke-recaller."

I smile, remembering how it felt for my words to flow so easily. How the judges clapped and asked questions about the equine therapy business I wanted to start, and how I answered every single one and the sparrows never woke up at all.

"I know I didn't win, but it almost seems like what happened is better," I say. It feels like looking at Pebble Mountain. Just like Dad said, there really is always another side.

Andy sticks his hands in his pockets and looks at his boots. "I agree. It's awesome, Little C."

I hand him Sam's water bucket. "You know I'm horrible at carrying water."

"You're not horrible." Andy takes the bucket from my hand. "I mean, you're pretty strong for a twelve-year-old." He scratches his neck with his other hand and looks down. "You're pretty strong in general."

I hear water rushing into the bucket as Andy holds it. And as I stand there listening to the droplets, filling what needs to be filled, I know he's right. I am strong.

But there's still something that bothers me.

"Andy," I say. "I don't want to be mad at you. But I really don't understand you."

Andy laughs. "Join the club. I'm still figuring myself out."

"No, seriously," I say. "I guess I can see why you liked Starshine. I mean, it was kind of annoying to read about people like Damian and Marie all the time, when I don't even know them, but Starshine in general sounded okay."

"Marie and Damian are my friends," Andy says. His voice sounds small somehow, like it did when he was younger. "I needed them. Starshine was helpful, but it was scary too, especially at first."

A sharp stab pierces me. I hadn't ever thought about Andy being scared. "I just don't get why you ended up there in the first place. Why you ever decided to—"

"Mess up like I did?" Andy asks.

It sounds harsh, but he doesn't seem to mind. He's smiling in an easy way, like he just figured out how to laugh at something that doesn't seem at first like it should be funny.

"Yeah," I say. "I guess that's it."

"It's a fair question." Andy looks up at the ceiling. Sighs. "Addiction is a disease, Claire. You probably heard that at your support group. I didn't choose it, but it affects me. It's something I have to keep working on, and I know how to do that now. Because of Starshine."

"But why did you start selling the pills?" I ask.

"It's hard to explain," Andy says. "I really needed to find a way to keep taking them. That's part of the disease."

"I don't understand why you needed them so much." I look at Andy, at his eyes part sparkling, part sad.

"You're my little sister," Andy says. "And you know me well, but you don't know everything. I struggle sometimes. Like with fitting in and doing what people want me to do. When I first started taking the pills, it didn't just make the pain go away, it also—made all those struggles go away too. I mean, obviously it made them worse later, but in the beginning at least, it seemed—I don't know. Helpful."

"It never seemed like you had problems fitting in," I say. "You always had so many friends." Andy never hated talking to people like I did. I couldn't picture a flutter feeling ever filling his chest.

But maybe he's right—maybe I don't know him as well as I thought I did.

"You can have friends without feeling one

hundred percent like yourself," Andy says. "That was me."

I don't know how it feels to be Andy. But thinking about having a problem like addiction, and fighting it, makes me realize I'm not the only one who's strong. He is too.

"When you left, I really wanted there to be some way for me to fix things," I say. "I wanted to make you like you were before."

"That's not up to you, Claire," Andy says. "If it were anybody's responsibility, it would be mine. But I don't *want* things to be like they used to be. I don't want to go backward."

"Neither do I." I'm surprised to find I really mean it. "Not anymore."

"I wanted to say something else too. I know I never explained all of this in my letters, but I just couldn't figure out how." Andy's voice cracks a little, but he runs his hands through his hair and keeps going. "I *am* sorry, Claire. I wish I didn't have this problem. I mean, I've learned a lot from it, but it's also really tough. Not just for me, but for you and Mom and Dad."

"It's been hard," I say. It feels important to say it out loud, just like Andy did. "But everyone has problems."

"I'm still sorry it didn't work out quite the way you wanted," Andy says. "Even though the whole equine therapy plan isn't right for me, I can see why it's perfect for you."

My big brother. Legs swinging from trees, sleeping bags under the stars. Wrenches and reins and wheels in his hands.

I stand on my tiptoes and reach my arms around his neck. His jacket smells like motor oil and hay. I don't want him to apologize. It feels good to really want Andy to do what's best for him. I can handle what's best for *me*. "You don't have to feel bad. You should do what you want to do. I just want you to be okay."

"Hey, I've got an awesome sister and some worry stones in my pocket," he says. "How can I go wrong?" There are questions in his voice, but his eyes look bright.

"So," he says, clearing his throat. "You figure Sunny's up for a ride?"

I'm surprised Andy wants to. He hasn't ridden in a long time, but that first snow melted fast and the sun's shining. "You think she can take both of us?" I ask. Sunny's big, but I don't think she's ever carried more than one person at a time.

"I bet she can handle a little walk in the woods," Andy says.

We lead Sunny out of her stall and Andy starts brushing her. "Let's go bareback," he says. "It's warmer that way, and besides, we can't both fit in the saddle. We'll make it quick."

I don't ride bareback often, so maybe I should feel nervous, but I don't. I just get Sunny's bridle.

Outside, Andy knits his palms together under my boot and gives me a boost onto Sunny's back. He hauls himself up behind me, and Sunny swings her head around, surprised, but she actually stands still.

"Good girl," I say, patting her neck. I'm laughing too, because Andy almost slides over the other side of Sunny, just before righting himself at the last minute.

Then we're moving forward, and the air's cold, but it feels good, fresh and clean and new. I turn my face up and catch sun on my skin. Sunny nods her head up and down, and her mane sparkles a little in the light.

Andy leans close to my ear. "Want to try and find some wild horses?"

I nudge Sunny toward the woods, where the dark trees bend together. The leaves are all gone now, colors fading into the ground. I can feel the pounding of hooves and the swish of silver-black tails, even though I can't hear or see them, not yet.

The start of a path unfolds before me, wild and true.

Where it leads is up to me.

AUTHOR'S NOTE

Claire's journey in *The Wild Path* was inspired by the millions of people who have been impacted by a loved one's struggle with the disease of addiction. The issue is widespread; in 2017 alone (the most recent year from which we have data), 19.7 million Americans aged twelve and older battled a substance abuse disorder[1]. Still, there is so much stigma and shame surrounding addiction—and it's up to all of us to break the silence by sharing experiences and telling stories like this one.

Addiction is widely recognized by the American Medical Association and other organizations as a disease. It's important to have sympathy for

---

[1] samhsa.gov/datareport/2017-nsduh-annual-national-report

people struggling with addiction, and to know that change is possible, while also recognizing the far-reaching negative impacts of this issue. Both those who battle addiction, like Andy, *and* their loved ones, like Claire, commonly feel anger, guilt, confusion, powerlessness, and other strong emotions. If you or someone you love shows signs of addiction, these resources might help:

- Alcoholics Anonymous (aa.org)
- Al-Anon (al-anon.org)
- Center on Addiction (centeronaddiction.org)

Claire also experiences anxiety, which can manifest in different ways for different people, with varying degrees of severity. If you think anxiety affects you, share your feelings with a trusted adult or a doctor. A trusted adult can also help you explore the following resources:

- Child Mind Institute (childmind.org)
- National Institute of Mental Health (nimh .nih.gov)

- Substance Abuse and Mental Health Services Administration Hotline: 1-800-662-HELP (4357)

The path to recovery is wide and long, but you need not walk it alone.

ACKNOWLEDGMENTS

The path a book travels from initial idea to finished product is indeed wild, full of surprising twists and turns and fueled by the persistence to continue moving forward. I am eternally grateful to the many people who helped bring *The Wild Path* into the world.

Thanks to Katie Grimm, my tireless agent: I'm so glad you're in my corner.

Lisa Yoskowitz and Hannah Milton, thanks as always for your keen editorial vision. Special thanks to Alexandra Hightower, who stepped in at a crucial time and guided Claire's story in important directions. I'm grateful to all of you for providing the patience, encouragement, and critical insight I needed. My appreciation extends to

Chandra Wohleber, Annie McDonnell, Alexander Kelleher-Nagorski, Christie Michel, and the entire Little, Brown publishing team for supporting this book. I absolutely love the breathtaking cover, so beautifully rendered by artist David Dean and designer Jenny Kimura.

Thanks to Jim Balmer, Jess Redman, Lisa Higgins, and Carrie Barker, readers and friends who offered professional expertise on mental health, addiction treatment, and equine therapy. Phillis Mosher, your encouragement means the world to me. Nicole Goldstein, you are the world's best critique partner. Stephanie Cohen-Perez and Nat Razi, I'm grateful for your thoughtful notes on characterization. Thanks also to Sergeant Kevin Cister of the Zeeland Police Department, who answered logistical questions; and Rory Carr, who clarified medical information.

I've been privileged to collaborate through the #KidsNeedMentors program with teacher extraordinaire Teri Kestner and her middle school students, who read an early draft of this book and offered valuable suggestions that I incorporated.

The Wild Path wouldn't be quite the same without these students—Izzy Goldenstein, Max Krus, Elizabeth Perry, and Mylie Waddill—who continually impressed me with their insights.

It feels impossible to count the forces that contributed to this story by fostering my love of reading, writing, family, and nature. From my parents, Don and Sharon Reinhard; to my brothers, Daniel and David Reinhard; to my neighbor Peg Metzger, who gave me a new book every Christmas Eve; to the many horses I rode and loved growing up, along with the teachers who helped me work with and care for them—including Gretchen Bittner, Carol Johnson, and the guides and instructors at Rainbow Ranch: Thank you for shaping my life.

Endless thanks go to my incredibly supportive, patient, and encouraging husband, Matthew, the strongest person I know. And to my children, Aaron and Joan, who have heard the sentence "Mama has to work a little longer on her book" too many times: I love you to the stars and back. You're the best of the best.

Turn the page for a sneak peek at

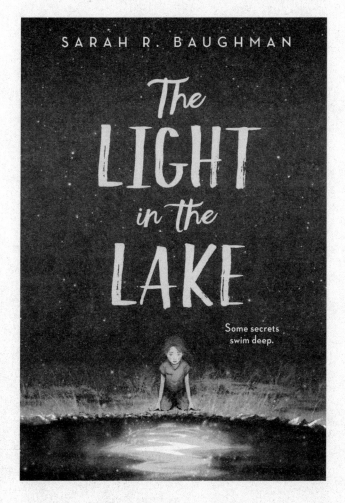

SARAH R. BAUGHMAN

The
LIGHT
in the
LAKE

Some secrets
swim deep.

Available Now

Chapter 1

School is all noise and lights—kids yelling, backpacks bumping. We have cinder block walls and metal doors so heavy they take forever to open, then clank shut too fast. Our lunchroom always smells like canned green beans. But I guess that's the good thing about school. It keeps going the way it is, even when nothing else does.

I walk through the hall with my head down, my shoulder bumping Liza's. She's my cousin, and also my best friend. She doesn't care how many times I bump her shoulder. Sometimes she touches her hand to my elbow, lightly steering me in the right direction.

Ten steps, I tell myself. *Ten... nine... eight...* I've been doing this a lot the past two months: staring at my feet, counting steps. I guess I just don't like thinking about all the kids trying *not* to look at me, their eyes full of whispers. My method works pretty well, except one time I walked right into a little kindergartner who had found her way into the middle school wing somehow. There's nine grades in this one building, and we're supposed to watch out for the littlest kids.

We make it to science and I exhale, fast.

Mr. Dale always stands outside his classroom door and sticks his hand out for us to shake as we walk in. I didn't think he'd keep that up past September, but it's the end of the year now and he's still going strong, pumping our hands up and down.

"Addie and Liza!" he says. "Welcome."

"Nice SpongeBob tie," Liza says; she's looking at me, holding a laugh in. We've both tried to figure out if he ever repeats a tie, or if he really has as many ties as there are days of school. This SpongeBob one is new. And pretty dorky.

Mr. Dale just smiles. "I'm glad you have such good taste. My son picked it out; apparently it's what all the Shoreland County preschoolers are wearing. Or wanting to wear."

Since it's almost the last week of school, most of the teachers have stopped giving us homework, but Mr. Dale's been making us chart the phases of the moon since May and he says there's no reason to stop before the full cycle's over. I realize as soon as Liza and the other kids start fishing their charts out of their backpacks that I forgot to look at the moon last night.

As Mr. Dale moves around the room checking work, he pauses just for a second and taps my desk with one finger. When I look down, I see a little yellow Post-it stuck there with a message written on it: *Deep breaths!* Then there's a smiley face with googly eyes, and his signature: *Mr. D.*

Teachers usually walk right by when I don't turn my work in these days, and they don't say anything. Mr. Dale is the only one who leaves little notes that make me feel like maybe someday I'll be okay.

"Your sketches are looking good," Mr. Dale tells the class. He picks Liza's up and puts it under the document camera. On the board, her drawings slide into focus; I can tell she used the dark charcoal pencils she got for her birthday.

"Liza," he says. "Could you please describe the moon you saw last night?"

"It's still a crescent," she says. "Smaller than two nights ago."

"Great," he says. "And why is it continuing to get smaller? It's a—what kind of crescent?"

Waning, I think, just as Liza says it. Waning: getting smaller and smaller until there's barely anything left. Liza's perfect crescent shimmers in the thick charcoal defining her night sky.

"That's kind of weird," I say. My own voice surprises me; the words sounded better when they were just thoughts, but it's too late to go back.

Mr. Dale nods, and I can tell it's the kind of nod teachers do when they want to include you in the conversation but they're not quite sure whether you're going to help it or ruin it. "How so, Addie?"

"Um…" I stall. Mr. Dale waits while the other kids start to fidget. "When you talk about seeing the moon, you mean the silvery glowing part."

"True," Mr. Dale says.

"But when you draw it on white paper, you can't actually *draw* that part." I look at the smudges Liza's charcoal pencils made. "You have to draw the dark part instead, and kind of use the dark part to show the light part." The words tumble out faster than my brain can really think them through. "So you're not actually drawing *the moon*. You're drawing the shadow that covers it up bit by bit until it looks like it was never there at all."

When I stop talking, the room's so quiet I can hear the wind outside, rattling young birch leaves together. Liza's just staring at me, her eyes big as full moons. The other kids stare too—kids I've known my whole life who have been trying really hard *not* to look at me since Amos died. Not wanting to look the wrong way, say the wrong thing. They don't know there *isn't* a right way. They might as well just look.

But Mr. Dale doesn't seem surprised. He just nods. "An excellent point, Addie," he says. "Scientifically and philosophically relevant. Darkness allows us to see light."

Liza sticks her hand up. She knows I don't like having all the focus on me, and she's probably thinking fast, trying to help. "You can sort of *see* the dark part too," she says. "I mean, it has a shape in the sky, if you really look."

"Can anyone predict when that darkness will cover the whole moon?" Mr. Dale asks. "When do you think this crescent will completely disappear and give us a new moon?"

"How about *never*?" In the back corner of the room, Darren Andrews snickers. I roll my eyes. Amos was Darren's friend—one of his only friends—since preschool.

When Darren was little, he'd get in trouble for spinning around in the teacher's chair when she got up to check assignments, drumming on his desktop, tickling other kids during story hour. We've never been close, but he used to at least nod at me in the halls, before. Now he just looks away like everyone else.

Mr. Dale sighs. "Darren," he says. "Let's have a little more faith in the moon. It's been around awhile. Anyone else?"

"A day?" someone asks.

"No way," says Liza. "We've got longer than that."

"Probably not much longer, though," says Mr. Dale. "Keep watching at night. See how long it lasts."

When class ends, Liza stays beside me instead of rushing out to the art room like she used to before Amos died. I zip my backpack—I know I'm taking too long, because Liza's eyes keep darting toward the clock, even though she'd never tell me to hurry—and sling it over one shoulder as I get up to leave.

"Addie," Mr. Dale says, pointing in my direction, "can I quickly touch base with you? I'll write you a pass to art."

I backtrack and stand next to his desk, waving Liza away. "I'll look at the moon tonight," I mumble in his direction. "I just sort of forgot last night. I—"

"It's not that," Mr. Dale says. "I'm just hoping you're planning to apply for the Young Scientist position we talked about."

I think of the crumpled Post-it note Mr. Dale put on my desk. Time to take that deep breath.

I missed a lot of school right after Amos died. So once I came back and Mr. Dale told me about the chance to spend this summer on Maple Lake, learning from scientists about how to study the water, I knew he was just trying to catch me up.

But I haven't known exactly how to feel about Maple

Lake. It used to be the place Amos and I both loved most. Now that he's gone, it feels different. It's a part of me that hurts to look at.

I won't say I didn't listen to Mr. Dale when he first mentioned the Young Scientist position. It's just that everything anyone said that month sounded like it was underwater. All the words gurgled, hard to hear, and most of them drowned somewhere outside me. I just couldn't hold on to them.

I look down at the papers scattered across his desk. "Um," I say slowly. "I've been..."

"...thinking about it?" he asks.

"I kind of have, but—" I twist my backpack strap around my fingers.

"You should consider it." Mr. Dale leans forward and shuffles the papers, then starts working through them with a pen. Maybe he knows I need some time to think.

As the Young Scientist, I would get to work at the biological station, a huge chunk of shoreline owned by the University of Vermont. Scientists go there to monitor water clarity and temperature, chart bird sightings, and study how cutting and using trees can keep the forest healthy. Amos and I used to play hide-and-seek on the nature trails there when we were younger.

"So...it's an everyday thing?" I ask.

"You bet," Mr. Dale says, still checking off papers.

"The researchers are there five days a week, and so am I, now that I'm studying for my master's. We'd like the Young Scientist to be there each weekday too."

Mr. Dale knows I want to be an aquatic biologist some-day. The one time I admitted it in homeroom, when we were supposed to talk about what we wanted to do when we grew up, most of the kids just stared.

But before I could figure out how to explain, Mr. Dale cut right through the silence and said that aquatic biologists can study not only the ocean, but freshwater lakes and rivers too, which is exactly what we have in Vermont, in between all the mountains.

"If you're accepted," Mr. Dale continues, looking up from his papers, "and everything goes well, you could join the Science Club next year, in seventh grade instead of eighth. We could make an exception."

That sounds pretty good to me. Science Club members get to ride the bus to the high school once a week to do cool experiments with the freshman earth science class.

"What's the project this summer?" I ask.

"We're looking at pollution levels in the lake," Mr. Dale says. He sets his stack of papers aside and folds his hands. "You could learn about testing water samples, entering data—"

"Pollution levels?" I feel my skin bristle. "Maple Lake's

not polluted. My dad says it's the coldest, clearest lake in the state."

"The water might look clear," Mr. Dale says, "but it's getting to the point where it isn't actually as clean as it might seem. Not according to some preliminary observations. And we want to know why." He looks right at me. "You've spent a lot of time on that lake."

Tears sting my eyes. Most people don't talk about Maple Lake with me anymore.

"It can't be easy," he says, his voice soft. "With . . . everything that happened."

I look up. *Say it*, I think. *Just say it. Nobody ever says it.*

As though he hears me thinking, Mr. Dale clears his throat. "With Amos," he says. "With your brother."

Hearing Mr. Dale say his name helps somehow. It's like the room had swelled to the point of bursting, a too-full balloon, and his name popped it. Everything settles, calms.

"I don't want to presume, Addie," Mr. Dale continues. "Working at the lake might not sound like the best idea to you. I just . . ." He trails off, looks up at the ceiling.

I clench the Post-it note so hard my fingernails dig into my palm. He's right, in a way. But the strange thing is—*not* working at the lake doesn't sound easy either.

Mr. Dale turns his palms up and shrugs. "Okay, look. I loved science when I was your age," he says. "When I became a teacher, I promised myself that if any of my students got as excited about it as I did, I'd help them out as much as I could. And this chance to study the lake seemed like an opportunity I should tell you about."

That's when I know for sure I really do miss Maple Lake. I feel it deep down, like water feels the wind pushing up waves. Mama and Dad and I haven't been there since *before*. But I don't think Amos would like it if I stayed away forever. And I realize now, I don't want to.

"If you applied, I think it could work out well," Mr. Dale says. "Scientifically speaking, you're a very strong candidate. You ask questions. And you think about things in different ways, like what you said about drawing the moon. Those are good qualities for a scientist to have."

I stand up a little straighter. "Thanks."

"Take this home," Mr. Dale says, handing me an application. "Talk about it with your parents. See what they say."

"I don't need to talk to them about it." I feel something inside pulling me toward Maple Lake now, even though it's the last place most people would expect me to go. "I'll apply."

Chapter 2

Liza and I line up for the bus together, arms linked, like always. I didn't tell her about the Young Scientist position at lunch or study hall. Not yet.

Liza was born just a couple of months before Amos and me. Sometimes Aunt Mary and Mama called us the triplets, and even though it wasn't technically true, it didn't quite feel wrong either. A lot of times I can tell what Liza's feeling, even when she's not saying a thing.

Like right now, I know she's thinking hard. Worried. She's chewing the side of her lip like she does when she's working on one of her sketches and thinks she messed it up but doesn't know how to fix it. She pulls me a little closer.

"Want to come over today?" she asks, quietly enough that nobody else can hear.

Amos and I used to go over to Liza's a lot after school. Her bus stop came before ours and Aunt Mary was always home by the time we got there, so if we knew Mama needed to sleep before work or Dad was still on a job site, it made sense. But I haven't been going over as much lately. Not since Amos died.

I wish I could explain this to Liza, but I don't even know if I can really understand it myself. Shouldn't I want to hang out with my cousin, the only other person who knew Amos close to as well as I did? The only person who wouldn't just stare at me with big, scared eyes if I started crying out of nowhere, or accidentally talking about Amos like he was still there?

"Um, I can't today." The words feel sharp, even though I don't mean them to be. "I have homework, and I think I need to start dinner because Mama's working…" The rest of the sentence wanders away. I don't need to look at Liza to know she's trying to look like everything's okay, like whatever I want is fine.

"No worries," she says. Our bus is pulling up, and Liza lets go of my arm as the doors heave open. My chest aches.

"Hi there, girls," Barbara Ann says from the driver's seat. "All aboard!" She takes one hand off the steering wheel to motion us up the steps, then winks one blue-shadowed eye.

Barbara Ann's one of Mama's best school friends and even babysat Amos and me sometimes when Aunt Mary couldn't, so I think I know her pretty well. I know you can count on her for a few things. Number one: frizzy brown hair that sticks out in places. She never pulls it back; it just falls all around her shoulders like milkweed fluff. Number two: bright red lipstick. Number three: gum, usually watermelon-flavored, and usually snapped between her teeth while she's talking, which she does a lot.

Snap. I guess there's a number four: the good mood. Barbara Ann really doesn't stop smiling, which comes in handy on days when I don't have the energy to do it myself. It reminds me of being little, learning to ride a two-wheeler: Mama would give me a little push on the back of the seat to get me started. Barbara Ann's smiles feel just like that.

"Hey, Barbara Ann," I say. And I make my lips go up at the corners.

She grabs my wrist. "Wait a second," she says. "Isn't tomorrow—"

"Yeah, I'll be twelve," I say. "Saturday. Guess I got lucky." The words taste sour. Pretending to be happy about a weekend birthday with no school seems stupid this year, but it also feels like a normal thing to say.

The nice thing about Barbara Ann's smiles is they aren't fake. When her lips kind of roll together, like they have to press hard to keep something else out, I can tell she's thinking about Amos and how he'll never be twelve. But her smile's still real. She looks right at me too, which is something people sometimes seem scared to do when they remember about Amos.

"You have a good birthday tomorrow, honey," she says. Then she reaches in her shirt pocket, pulls something out, and presses it into my hand.

"Found this," she whispers. "An early present. Keep it safe." I walk toward the back of the bus and find my seat by Liza just as Barbara Ann shifts into gear and we roll away.

"What did she give you?" Liza leans over, trying to catch a glimpse of my hand.

"I don't know." The thing, whatever it is, is smooth, curved, with a sharp point. I don't want to open my hand, though. When I realize I'm waiting for Amos to come so he can see whatever it is too, tears start and I have to blink hard. Liza hooks her hand through the crook of my elbow, pulls me a little closer on the seat.

I picture Amos across the aisle, leaning over for a closer look. "*Open it!*" he'd whisper, loudly enough for me to know he meant it. But of course if he were here, he'd probably have one too. He would already know what it was because he never would have been able to wait.

I let my fingers open and there it is: white, quarter-moon-shaped. Perfect.

"A tooth?" Liza's nose wrinkles. "Has Barbara Ann completely lost it?"

"It's a white whale tooth." I would know one anywhere; Amos and I love—loved—to collect them. Over ten thousand years ago, the Atlantic Ocean flooded over land pressed low by glaciers, and white whales swam right through it. Only when the land rose back up, filling with fresh water draining off the mountains, did the whales go away. Even so, they left evidence of themselves: one of their skeletons turned up in a farmer's field over in Charlotte a long time ago, and now it's our state fossil. "But it's a really big one. Huge, actually. Almost—" I stop.

"Almost what?"

"Nothing." I shake my head. There are some things I don't want to tell even Liza. Like how if Amos were here, he'd say there was no way a white whale could have this big a tooth, that it had to come from somewhere—something—else. Like the creature, swimming through the deepest parts of Maple Lake.

It wasn't really like Amos to keep secrets, but I know he didn't say anything about the creature to anyone else, not even Liza. He wanted to prove it first. *"You're a scientist, Ad,"* he said. *"You can help."*

But I didn't believe him.

SARAH R. BAUGHMAN

is a former middle and high school English teacher who now works in curriculum development. Sarah graduated from Grinnell College and the University of Michigan, then went on to teach English overseas. After spending a number of years in rural northeastern Vermont, she moved back to Michigan with her husband and their two children. *The Wild Path* is her second work for young readers; she is also the author of the middle-grade novel *The Light in the Lake*. Sarah invites you to visit her online at sarahrbaughman.com.